Flux & the Void

ISBN 978-0-578-41334-1

Cover Art by: Ruben Rodriguez

Flux & the Void

Written by

Johnny Lee Chapman, III

For Danielle M. Coulter

"Live outside the box"

Table of Contents

Farewell to Humanity (I)

2 | Flux & the Void

It is stated that words may forget the writer, but *the writer will never forget the words*. If true, then curse my ill fate for there are sentences I wish to permanently banish from my memories. Yet I find it strangely compelling that I initially desired to conceal my identity from you, brave reader. The first page of any literary endeavor should be addressed to the author, and who more qualified to write such an admission than said author. Perhaps my ardent desire for catharsis is what initially pushed my pen to the page; therefore, I have concluded to share the current state of my affairs-it will certainly aid in your acceptance of the forthcoming address.

I am Flux.
I reside in the **Void***.*

Here, in the **Void**, impossibility is a fleeting idea. There is no form, logic, or reasoning to the **Void**. It simply is, and will continue to be, *indefinitely*. I fear there are but few adjectives I could use to describe it…but realize it is more than a location: The **Void** is alive.

It exists as a singular unit comprised of cells devoured by a cosmic horror from the dark of the universe. Think of it as a dimensional plane rebirthed through the eons, retaining the consciousness of an ancient being. I do not know if the **Void** has always been my home, or if I recently arrived; how I came to be sentient in this ominous vacuum is beyond my comprehension. Personal details regarding my past life remain nonexistent-what is life but a rudimentary speck of divinity in a sea of dark matter? But I do not bother toying with pieces of the past, rather I pursue my purpose. I exist to impress the present upon these pages.

What I am about to confess are tales of wonder, of fright, of truths greater than the understanding of science and skepticism. Tales of the entities, or residents of the **Void**-under the assumption the definition of entity is a being with an independent existence. For the duration of this anthology, I will refer to them as such, for I am unable to classify them as anything else-they are so atypical to anything your race has encountered.

The entities have visited your planet for millennia, before the germination of elements and molecules. Now, they materialize in forms not limited to the traditional vessel; some are known to don human skin. I've even recorded a rare incident of a lifeform tearing through the Schism, a fabric layer of space-time that separates dimensional planes, and invading in their authentic form. Their mystery is only matched by their unbound power as you, brave reader, will come to understand.

For an undistinguished amount of time (humans are so primitive with linear temporality) I have diligently studied a diverse array of entities and collected empirical information regarding their arcane nature. This book is a culmination of what answers I have obtained...thus far. The stories transcribed in this anthology are *of my own pen*. Every word written is a moment once observed, and I attempted to recreate that reality as best as I could-writing is not a practice taught in the Void.

Now that I have shared the catalyst behind this compilation, *I must warn you*...it is in your best interests to remain wholly ignorant of the Void. And what resides within it. Whenever one of you humans becomes too involved with an entity, self-destruction soon follows, and I'd rather not bear witness to any unnecessary sorrow.

As a documentarian I will not withhold any information, for truth must be known for it to have power. Providing this unfiltered story may help you, curious reader, prepare if an entity should ever appear; so, *believe everything that is written*. If you choose to read, then you are solely responsible for whatever conclusion your imagination creates.

I've been told that introductions can last an eternity; however, immortality is not yet known to your kind. Since time is limited, I will not delay any further...but there is one final topic I must address.

As a witness, I stayed my hand whenever danger appeared...I did not wish to disrupt to the natural boundary between our dimensions by intervening. The recorded misfortunes are indeed tragic, but you humans are aware that death awaits, and any endeavors to alter fate is foolhardy.

Do not think ill of me; I am merely a vessel for the Void. It is my duty to record the truth, no matter how fantastical, or frightening.

Encounter

6 | Flux & the Void

Ah, I have noticed your eye, this photograph interests you, doesn't it? Upon first glance, it is merely a woodland shrouded in shadows, thickets cast with creatures who come alive in the night. But there's more to it, and that is why you continue to look. Even when you browsed through the other images, some that have even been featured in the MoMA, some that capture the fleeting kiss of beauty, this photo is the one. The one that invades your peripheral, haunts the view from every angle. Closing your eyes doesn't help, because it soon appears in the blackness beyond the eyelids. So, you open them again, and you face it, because there is something that you need to know. It's melded within the subject, the frame, even the woodland. Ominous, right? What is it? Allow me to share a woeful tale of disaster and discovery to you who gaze upon my famed photograph. It is the duty of the artist to enlighten the common citizen; this I do by art.

Now, art is subjective and can be classified as many things, but *the one thing it cannot be is a lie*. And this print, this image that beckons your undivided devotion, is art. Come, let me reveal to you the backstory behind this print, which I have named: *The* Scleridite.

**

Apprehension. Fright. Terror.

What dreadful delight I am delivered when shocks shoot down the nape of my black neck as if Tesla's lightning surged through my skin. This feeling, this expression of the subconscious is but a mere smidgen of raw fascination. Of an experience with the sublime that has forever altered the course of the soul operating this rotting body. You may curiously wonder as to why I describe my countenance as rotting, as to which I'd simply reply: *we live to die.*

Whenever faced with death, which is always, humans find a way to overcome the odds and embrace a sense of life-and, scientifically speaking, our cells decompose daily. As a young boy, I was no stranger to these primordial feelings of fear, accepting them as my ordained masters rather than joy or comfort. This may indeed come as somewhat of a surprise to those who had the opportunity to behold me in my boyhood; my childhood was relatively free of suffering and anguish. Both of my parents worked their way towards the middle class and were employed in stable positions.

Their labor led to the purchase of a beautiful two-story home on the outskirts of a town with a name nearly impossible to pronounce-except by the locals. I spent my formative years here, and it was within these walls that I discovered that caustic emotion: fear.

Seven is a unique age for a child raised in the South, and I was more curious than any starving country coon. Sneaking around the house while my parents performed chores, learning about the world by experiencing it firsthand. I touched everything to know its texture, angled my eyes to both the soil and sky rather than straight ahead, and even tasted things I knew were probably not meant for consumption. During the summer I blossomed, as I was instructed to remain outdoors, which only furthered my budding desire for knowledge. The days under the blazing sun spent playing with magnifying glasses, slaying imaginary beasts with sticks, and twirling through the sprinkler system were everything to me. If I had even a sliver of the wisdom I now contain, I would have left the unknown alone and removed this thorn of fear from my life; but alas time travel is, at present, still a modern myth.

Although my family had almost two acres in their name, nearly all of it, except for the house, was covered by a dense forest. The trees stretched beyond the reaching of my naive eyes, beyond the bramble bushes tangled in Hangman's knots. Behind our property line was an inaccessible zone, or so I had been told since birth. But, as all seven-year-olds do, I believed myself ready to conquer nature.

Foolish.

Upon waking on the morning of a humid Saturday in the North Carolina countryside, I was tasked with helping my father with his outdoor activities. We cut the front and back lawn (about 0.5 acres), washed the family cars, trimmed the overgrown shrubbery next to the porch, threw pine straw and mulch around the garden, and scrubbed the dog with anti-tick shampoo.

Normally, our routine lasted until four in the afternoon, but on this fated day we happened to finish before lunch, thus granting a free day. With the rest of the day ahead of me, I began what may have become my first act of preparation.

Another summer day of exploration in the woods. My bosom was filled with an expected timidity, and I do remember there was some anxiety, but these emotions soon faded. I longed for whatever laid beyond the edge of the property line; a primal passion awakened within me, a feeling that I'd only experienced while riding my bike without holding the handles. A sense of life, if you will. I looked to the forest for my freedom, but what laid within the thicket was far from liberty.

Hustling upstairs with the fervor of a hunter contracted to a new bounty, I procured my blue Batman book bag (*The Caped Crusader* is favorite hero of every 90's child) from my closet, a beach towel that doubled as a blanket, an industrial strength yellow flashlight, and a disposable camera (one always needs proof when dealing with the unknown). Before I set out, I savored the last bit of sandwich made by my mother's hands; how delicious her meals had been when I retained my innocence, ignorant to the existence of the *other world.*

The world of the forest. A realm of bark and rotting wood, a secret that nature had purposely intended to keep from man; yet here I was, a seed of Adam, approaching with brevity, and tickled by the scent of pine straw. I cannot adequately recall a distinct entrance, for the forest sprawled from the street to behind the wooden gates my father erected. I wandered through shrubbery, stepping upon ages of dead foliage decomposed by fungal spores. With the light at my back, I managed to photograph striking silhouettes of the stumps, how they resembled headless bodies half buried in the dirt. My disposable camera continued to click and click, and with each snapshot, I sank farther into the dense woodland.

Intimate details regarding the journey are hazy, but my situation changed from curious to cautious as I lost the path back home. How many hours were spent in this organic expanse of land I may never truly know; I vividly remember watching the sun starting to disappear behind the decaying leaves. Night drew closer and the structure known as my home was lost beyond the mass of towering evergreen.

Now, there are two types of forests: the normal variety with vegetation and insects, and then there is the forest after dark, which is more acquainted with alien biomes and Grecian labyrinths. The chirping of crickets became the screeching of buried sirens, vines slithered, and fungal nooses hung from branches. It was as if the darkness were made physical-I dare say, if I extended my hand, I would have touched something. However, my hands were occupied with holding onto the flickering yellow flashlight for dear life.

There was a rustle underneath the bed of leaves, a tapping of paws against the loamy soil, and for a brief second, I was entreated to the whisper of nocturnal beasts. Low, inaudible growls that originated from every direction, even above, filled the air while light faded. Dead branches raked at each other like rabid animals, and the wind cut through the lifeless leaves swirling like bones hung on a chime. My poor senses, they were mere pawns at the mercy of the vengeful forest. In my state of panic, I imagined the trees coming to life and forming a massive barrier, isolating me from the entire world. Loneliness constricted my neck as nature reminded me of man's eternal curse: *death is a solitary experience.*

Realizing that I'd failed to replace the batteries in my flashlight after the most recent summer storm, I was left with no choice but to make a mad dash in whatever direction seemed the easiest to traverse. My feet carried my body through the shadows, arms scraped by clawing branches as I navigated fallen trees and patches of thicket halting my progress.

Until a decaying root caught the bulk of my boot and sent my frame crashing into a bed of thorns.

Although blessed with natural intuition I was not a dexterous child, escaping from the thorn bush without injury was impossible. By the time I was set free, the remaining voltage from my flashlight battery was drained and cuts decorated my arm. Indeed, the suddenness of the accident shocked me but even as my eyes welled, my heart had yet to fully taste the nectar of the macabre

Placing my thumb underneath my tongue, I tasted blood.
My blood.

Rich in iron, but detestable in flavor; I quickly spat the liquid upon the bark of the neighboring tree. As I stood in this overgrown temple, surrounded by the sentinels of the earth, my budding soul cried out in despair: had I met my end in the forest? I remember tearing through the frightening woods, with my blue book bag double strapped around my shoulders, before my progress was halted by a sight so mysterious my brain misinterpreted the sensation, rendering me immobile.

What is our obsession with *light*? To seek the light is to leave shelter. By following illumination, we were expelled from the comfort of our mother's womb, removed from the cave of Plato. Perhaps it is not the dark…but the light we should fear.

Off in the distance, beyond a nestle of contorted branches appeared *three glowing orbs*, positioned in a triangle formation, hovering almost six feet above the damp bed of the forest. The luminance partially disoriented my vision, the same way one momentarily loses sight while staring directly at the sun. Unable to accurately analyze the strange occurrence, for the shrieks of the hidden creatures were growing *ravenous*, I wept. My eyes leaked like the cut upon my finger, slow and laden with sorrow.

As I tasted this crimson substance once more, I exchanged glances with the three orbs. It's a bit crazy to admit, but it felt as if I were the one being examined, like a black lab rat stuck as a specimen in an extraterrestrial experiment conducted behind the pool of shimmering light. Strangely enough, the spheres weren't just bright, they were in motion as well. Being a child of the outdoors, I have spent many breezy sunsets by the pond; when I stared upon these lights before me, I saw the waves dancing with the rays in a similar fashion.

I can't say for how long I ran through the woods, but throughout my sprint, I always saw the three lights. Their position never stayed the same, appearing on both left and right side of the forest as if teleporting. There was a change in air pressure, barely noticeable by adults-as children we are more sensitive to forces; I imagine if the gravity of the earth was changed but two decimal points, it would feel somewhat like this. My tongue felt numb, and instead of profusely sweating, my arms shivered like they did in the snow.

A pungent stench emanated from the dark, engulfing the entire forest-my stomach lurches even now thinking about it. Its odor was that of cremation chimneys, sodium bicarbonate (household bleach), and, strangely enough, the *wax of honeybees*.

What ecstasy I felt, an experience that can't be explained in words. My nerves overloaded, and each node fired in sync. These sensations soon, however, festered from fascination to fright; cast out of the illusion of pleasure, I realized that there was no logical explanation for these lights. Which, to a seven-year-old, is a clear sign of danger.

Agony found me a viable vessel and screams of terror escaped my lips. My mind consciously wandered while my body continued the escape route, but what of my soul? What was that pin needle prickling in my chest? This sensation, this magnificent rush of adrenaline and anguish. It propelled my being into depths that I never knew existed. Swimming from a surface light that held nothing but sorrow.

It was fear.

My lungs burst as I slowed to a light jog once again, for the orbs had stopped pursuing…and fear relieved itself from my body through the form of urine. I was heading to, what I perceived to be, the lights of my back porch; but my ordeal became more harrowing when I happened upon a running creek.

The current carried water from west to east, or north to south...maybe it is best to say from one direction to the next, for I had no account of my location. I must mention that a creek was not in our property, which meant I was beyond the line, in the inaccessible zone- truthfully, I was unaware this body of water existed until that very moment.

A lone leaf sailed down the makeshift river, this tranquil sight momentarily calmed my hypersensitive nerves. The serenity was, unfortunately, broken by an ominous humming.

An exquisite melody full of innocence and sorrow; even my savage ears tickled at the presence of this tune. Its exact origin I could not precisely pinpoint, but it echoed as if it were quite far. I witnessed pitches and notes not heard in even the most established of symphony halls. Once I read that bats caught their prey by utilizing sonar waves, but as a child I was ignorant to the hunting rituals of beasts. No, this noise sounded coherent, lucid...*alive.* What happened next remains a mystery, for I cannot recall the logic of choice behind my actions (if one believes in free will).

I whistled.

My lips pursed in the same fashion that my father had recently taught me, and I harmonized with the eerie tune. An artistic expression of emotions filled the thicket as the duet, or choir, or solo echoed.

As my tongue tasted the notes of the tune, I was entreated with my favorite sights: freshly unearthed dinosaur fossils, stars discovered with telescopes, a blue-ringed octopus swimming in the tidepool, photographs of my parents' faces. How such a performance made me witness these memories I cannot say, but it was as if my fate had been transcribed into a concerto.

This passion continued to burn for a few ecstatic moments until the last visible will-o-wisp of the sunset was replaced by the twilight. Afterwards, I realized that I was the only thing making noise, and when I stopped, my ears were greeted with the yawning of the slumbering earth. The chattering creatures went silent and the wind failed to produce a rustle, even though it tumbled through the leaves before my very eyes.

My favorite vegetables were carrots, which I must thank for my excellent night vision; but in this moment I failed to register anything except the three lights, which were now shining brightly on the opposing side of the bank. Water splashed, but the droplets did not fall back to the creek. They remained afloat in mid-air, warping into condensed spheres.

The first orb shifted an inch to the left, and my breath ran icy cold despite it being midsummer. Before I had time to react, the right orb moved in the opposing direction, followed by the top which dropped to the ground. In an instant, all three came to the imaginary center and leaves from the highest branches glided to their graves. A weighted thump then shook the earth, the epicenter somewhere near the bank covered in foliage.

Frozen by terror, my legs gave out and I, once again, found myself intimate with the forest floor. The three lights stopped moving, pulsed twice, and vanished in the blink of an eye. Again, I was alone at the edge of the bank. Rising to my feet with fear and determination as my guides, I hurriedly set off in the opposing direction of the creek; surely my destination did not lie on the other side of the river and I dared not discover the origin of those strange bulbs. Unfortunately, at this time in my life, I had yet to discover Greek mythology or I would've known of the fate of Orpheus, and nothing good ever comes from peering over the shoulder.

The luminous orbs returned to the bank, except this time there was a fourth, significantly larger sphere located directly in the center of the smaller ones. It resembled a wrecking ball; exhibiting similar properties as the other bulbs. The hue of this orb was a deep navy, and its light illuminated the neighboring trees. As the three continued to revolve around this massive puddle of floating light, a bellow erupted from the sky above.

Hovering in the position of the lights was a malformed shape. I fear that words would ultimately be useless to describe the silhouette that my eyes witnessed; suffice to say there was *no trace of humanity* in any of it. The same melody I unconsciously recognized returned, but this time it was accompanied by dispassionate gargle, echoing from the **Void** within the fourth orb.

This next confession may seem imaginary, but as an artist, I have no desire to do anything but share the truth behind my art. The thicket to my left rustled and I pivoted while keeping my eyes locked on the strange display of luminance. A cicada broke the melody, and both me and the figure simultaneously shifted in response to this noise. The leaves beneath my feet started to rise upwards like helium balloons. Blood seared as it flowed through arteries. I quickly detached myself from the book bag and dove away from the creek, then crawled through the chilled mud until my back met the bark of some fallen tree. The book bag, my favorite bag that held my adventure tools was now *suspended* in mid-air, along with the contents hanging directly below it.

An arm-like appendage covered in thick hair exited from the abyss of blue light and rummaged through my floating belongings. A mass of yellow flesh (if it could be called such), oozed from the base of the arm. The drippings lazily drifted to the earth like ashes, and the leaves burst into smoke. I witnessed a set of what I'd call...fingers, take hold of my flashlight. Somehow, this thing managed to click the power button, and a beam shot out of the lens; however, it didn't travel very far because it was refracting against something above me.

An eye.

A massive, corporeal oculus appeared inches above the orbs. Grotesque and enlarged, it was texturized with the cloudiness found in the irises of cadavers. Instead of a circular pupil, seven lines formed a hexagon. The silent figure did not remain steady for long, the eye blinked. And when it did, the luminance from the flashlight disappeared, as if swallowed by a black hole.

I was but a slave, and fear was my master! But is that not when man's power shines? When they must oppress the master? This thing had yet to discover me, but being a child of Eve, I dared to commit a forbidden act for the sake of knowledge.

Moving with the precision of a sniper, I loaded my camera, adjusted the lens to my liking, and took a deep breath of the forest air. A quick burst of light temporarily blinded me, and the orbs reacted similarly.

A metallic shrill filled the air, a whine that sat in the base of one's inner ear, becoming increasingly louder as I laid perfectly still. The horrid stench returned. Suddenly, three smaller appendages sprung forth from the original orbs and gripped the edge of my flashlight. The eye and the larger orb headed towards my direction. As they neared, I threw my camera around my wrist and hid behind the log. Soil coated my cheeks as I held my mouth shut.

The thumping stopped, and slowly the whine receded. Cautiously crawling over the log, I observed the eye return to the three smaller orbs, ending its search in a disorienting flash of magenta.

The appendages retreated to the depths like a turtle seeking refuge within its shell, leaving me horrified and soaked in urine. The mass of flesh was now a puddle of melted, azure slime with a similar constitution to ectoplasm. Prismatic colors puddled together as luminous spheres danced around the forest, and the silhouette of the abominable eye dissolved into the darkness of the tree-line.

My flashlight crashed on the forest floor. I immediately dashed to inspect it but halted after noticing the primordial slime corroding the metal handle. And my book bag was gone; oh, how I loved that satchel.

The presence of the strange orbs could no longer be felt, and I realized this was my opportunity to find the back porch. I made one final attempt at locating my bearings, finally utilizing the darkness to my advantage. In the distance, through a bramble of thickets, I saw an orange light flickering on and off.

The signal for curfew.

Adrenaline provided my legs with enough strength to propel me from this creek, all the way back to the exterior of the wooden gate. When I opened the iron latch on the back gate, I dropped on my back and stared skyward. The forest was back to normal, or perhaps this was normal for the wooded areas. Maybe I was the unexpected one, the intruder on a sacred ritual conducted under the veil of twilight.

Although shaken, I was safe.

Shortly afterwards, I found refuge in the bathtub on the second story of my home; the warm water cleansed my body, but even now there are nights when my dreams are haunted by that terrifying encounter with, "the Scleridite".

**

"And this photograph is the image of this...thing in the forest? This Scleridite?" A middle-aged woman with olive oil skin inquired while inspecting the frame.

The artist tickled the name badge on his hip. "Developed from the disposable camera from the story. I've included it in every exhibit I've partaken in: from Milan, to Thailand, and even here in Switzerland. Hoping maybe another patron will recognize it, and possibly shed some light."

"Mhhm, I see. Well for abstract art, I do say this piece is immaculate."

"Your compliments are far too kind, madam Chloi. I included a copy of it in the bundle you purchased," he humbly bowed.

"And your tale, most exciting. I love a good man-versus-nature story. Only recently, my husband and son became separated by a minor avalanche when hiking a small summit in the Alps. My sweet Canas was all alone, stranded for hours. Miraculously, he found us. Thankfully, we are in the warm season, or I fear we'd be having a different conversation."

"I'm pleased to hear he is safe."

"He may be young, but he is quite the resourceful one. He returned to us with no bruises or broken bones, but the experience has somewhat...shaken him up. Hopefully hearing your tale will help the boy muster some courage," she petted the head of the timid youth hiding behind her dress. "I fear I'm beginning to ramble, and I know how dreadfully boring my monologues can sometimes be. I bid you adieu, I look forward furnishing my home with some of these exotic pieces." Chloi lifted her frilled black dress and trotted away with her designer bag.

The enigmatic artist fumbled through the metallic cash box as he began whistling a serene melody. While the madame who introduced herself as Chloi packed her cheque book, a curious set of eyes poked from behind her legs and turned to the artist. A boy no older than eight with bronze hair cut into a bowl, dressed in a wool sweater tucked into a pair of overalls. In his hand he carried a foot-long baby blue flashlight while his left was tightly clutching his mother's dress.

Taking note of his gaze, the artist cheerily waved but his gesture received no response; as if the child were caught in an illusion that the artist, alone, somehow understood.

The boy's gaze was filled with curiosity, wonder, and...*fear*.

A quick tugging of the arm by his mother removed Canas from the mirage, and the mother-son couple made for the exhibit's food hall, but not before the young boy flickered his flashlight in the artist's face.

Nightfall

"Now, now gentlemen, please be gentle with these canvases, I've paid a small fortune for them." Chloi directed the movers.

"Where do you want us to hang this one up?"

"Next to the mantle, please. I think this will look great with the other pieces in here. There's a theme, I'm just not sure what it is yet," Chloi tapped her lip.

"And this one?" one of the moving men grunted while dabbing a bead of sweat.

"Leave that in storage, it's a fraud. Only authentic pieces will be visible in my home." The photograph was kept in its sealing and placed on the side of the woman's recliner couch.

A timid voice broke through the chatter of the moving men. "But Ma, that's a real photo. Those are the fairies."

"What fairies, dear?"

"The fairies I saw on the big mountain, when me and Pa got lost."

"Canas…darling, don't be delirious. Not only are there no such things as fairies, but this photograph is obviously a fake. It was taken halfway across the world…by an American. *You can't trust them.*"

She knelt down and brought her son's soft cheeks to her face, "I told you Canas, those lights were other hikers. They were using glowsticks to search for you. Not fairies."

With a pout upon his face the young boy pulled his head away and sulked in the corner of the regal living room. The four walls were covered with impressionist style paintings, bookshelves containing names from Moses to Nietzsche and Kepler; marble sculptures of angels sat on the corner of the end table.

"But he must know the fairies because he has a picture of them; he knows their songs too."

"Canas, why don't you go read? Then, go to sleep, please. I'll come in to say goodnight." Chloi unzipped her riding boots and neatly placed them next to the shoe shelf in the hallway closet. However, Canas was on the verge of tears, upset that his claims were being ignored (as most children's claims are).

"Can we please put the picture up? In my room?" he pleaded with his blonde haired, hazel-eyed mother.

"How about we put it in the hallway, just outside of your room? Your father would scold me like a schoolgirl if you were to get nightmares from it."

"Okay!" With cheer, the boy sprinted into his room; Chloi embraced the smile that arrived upon his face. She ordered the movers to find a place for the photo before returning to the master bedroom to don something more comfortable.

The age of Chloi Glaus dramatically shifted depending upon her wardrobe; nearly forty-five, she often got mistaken for a graduate student while wearing her tailored pieces around the campus she taught at-cashiers often ID'd her when purchasing wine. As she shed her clothes, the mother unhooked the golden locket hung around her neck, glanced at the picture inside, and brought the accessory close to her bosom.

"He's safe. *He's safe.*"

She placed the pendent in the jewelry box then went into the bathroom, where she would brush and water floss while showering. With wet hair wrapped in a cotton towel, she tiptoed into the hallway. She retrieved her glass of aged Cabernet Sauvignon from the shelf in the library and gulped a hearty portion while wandering to the staircase. The clicking of her slippers against her heels momentarily stopped; hung on the wall, above a white cedar end table holding her husband's phonograph, was the print purchased from the enigmatic artist.

The photograph appeared relatively normal: the trees obscured the horizon, and the creek below reflected the light from the flash. However, the image was well composed, and encouraged the mind to form its own conclusion. Technically it fit the criteria for art, and thus, deserved a place in her home. Removing her finger from the frame, the woman quickly gulped down the entirety of her glass and was about to retire to the master bedroom when a faint lull escaped her son's bedroom door.

At first it was nearly inaudible, like a gargle; but it slowly evolved into a rhythmic tune. Her son had been advancing in his piano lessons, but this melody was beyond notes and scores; this echoed from a great distance, in some far cry realm where man's science and theories were useless.

The wine glass exploded on the floor as recognition finally dawned on the woman; the song was the same tune whistled by that eccentric American.

Suddenly, the photograph developed an eerie luster; sharpened details sprung forth from the inked matte and the dense thicket suffocated the hallway, leaving Chloi gasping for air. Her body slid down the opposing wall. With eyes deadlocked onto the image, ardently examining the pixelated thorn bushes for any signs of life. The humming abruptly stopped; Chloi shrieked as her eyes finally registered the appearance of an apparition.

Enlarged legs like that of a tarantula jutted at angles, an oblong-shaped eye, a sickly thin tentacle with a strange fluid oozing out of a pore onto a mass of steaming flesh. The azure mass of viscous matter drained the saturation from the image.

The eye blinked. And then it looked at her.

Her sight was glued to the frame, as if patiently waiting for the figure to spring to life from the ink. The grotesque figure remained burnt into her imagination and appeared in greater detail when she shut her eyes. When she opened them phantom within the photograph had disappeared

Or...it was never there.

A blood curdling shriek escaped her throat, for across the closed blinds of the hallway window was a strange pulsing of lights. The beams rotated in a circle; three, small orbs waltzing across her ceiling. Growing larger, the spheres stopped moving near the light fixture. Seconds later, a police siren wailed from the street-crime was rare in Bern, but the occasional robbery brought law enforcement out every few months.

Chloi sprinted into the bedroom and awakened Canas. The orbs disappeared as the echoes of the siren grew more distant, but the woman was not convinced they were alone within their home. As the commotion dissipated, she unhinged her son. Canas gathered himself, but not without being showered with kisses. Her unexplained outburst terrified the poor child. Flashlight in hand, he said not a word and went back to his bed. Gently, Chloi closed the door behind her as she exited, and once again the woman was alone in the dimly lit corridor.

With the photograph.

Humored by the false scare, Chloi retrieved the bits of glass from the floor. Slightly tipsy from the wine, she accidentally nicked her thumb on a shard. Although barely visible, the wound oozed profusely; she brought the finger to her mouth since there were no wrappings in the vicinity. The air in the hallway was stagnant, and a foreboding darkness engulfed the corridor, leaving only trace amounts of light bleeding from her son's bedroom.

"Art is subjective; it can be classified as many things,
but the one thing it cannot be is a lie."

The photograph beckoned her, and despite the initial judgement, she relented by approaching. Her eyes traced the dense thicket once more before coming to the right corner, staring intently at the signature upon the image. If the artist's tale were true, and this photograph was proof of it, then how could she deny it? There was no need for the man to spin such a tale just to increase the value of the edit; and, although American, his aura was one of rustic virtue. And an artist, for his work caused her mind to capsize.

Chloi searched the image for the being, the Scleridite, but its form failed to produce this time. The light in her son's room extinguished, and the hallway was pitch black, enshrouding the frame in darkness. The blood from her wound stopped flowing and Chloi carried the shards in her hand, until one of them reflected a deep violet against the decorative walls.

Unable to immediately determine the origin of the luminance, Chloi inspected the fragments first. After finding out that they were, indeed, regular shards of an Ikea glass, her hair stood on edge. The wine that was housed within the cup was also too dark to resemble the painted below hue. She turned, and her face displayed a shock comparable to individuals tasked with identifying a loved one in a morgue. Casting from underneath the base of her son's door was a ray of blue light dancing upon the shards.

The door burst open, and Chloi immediately dove for Canas' bed even though the darkness had made it near impossible to see. Her fingers ran through her son's hair and she felt the clamminess of his skin; however, the slight thump of his bird chest calmed her nerves-only slightly. Chloi shielded her son's eyes; he need not witness this haunting occurrence, lest his nightmares intensify. His flashlight then powered on, the beam firing directly into her eyes.

Beams from the flashlight whizzed across the covers, bathing the walls as a prison searchlight would during a riot. Floating near the ceiling was an oversized sphere of undulating light, glowing like magma erupting from a dormant volcano. In a flash of magenta, the chandelier bulbs burst, as well as any electronic device within the vicinity, except the flashlight, which ran on disposable batteries.

The woman kept her lips sealed, but her son who was still in shock from his disappearance began to violently shout. The atmosphere became thick with anxiety, and the ambiance dissolved into silence. Chloi couldn't hear her labored breathing, nor the scream of Canas-despite his mouth being wide open

Chloi rubbed her eyes, and that's when Canas saw them. The fairies.

A shape revealed in the darkened bedroom, an oval-shaped mass of...something suspended in mid-air. She shifted positions to the floor and instructed her child to quickly hide underneath the bed, which he did without any hesitation. The shadows hanging above writhed like a web of serpents and out of the blackness appeared the clouded eye.

Chloi felt its gaze turn upon her. The large orb of light pulsed violently, nearly triggering a seizure. A hair-like appendage slithered out of the **Void**, and it patted the mattress of the twin-sized bed as if it were searching. Or rather...*hunting*. The artist's tale was true; this apparition, this otherworldly monstrosity unbound to physics or elements...this Scleridite was real.

Defenseless, and still in utter disbelief, Chloi remained immobilized by fear, save for her eyes which were constantly seeking any recognizable shape upon the being. A frigid chill coursed through her veins, although she was sweating profusely; if possible, she would've flayed her own skin. Her hallucination was finally broken by the sniffling of her son. Noises returned, but the overloading senses prevented her brain from registering any sound.

The Scleridite suddenly stopped moving.

Small objects in the room rattled; the Glaus family watched as their hair rose toward the ceiling. Along with toys, trophies, and the *comforter* protecting them. Within seconds, every piece of furniture under fifteen pounds was suspend in mid-air, perfectly still.

Canas laid curled into a ball, with tears and other bodily fluids leaking out of every orifice. Reflexively, Chloi shielded her son and prepared him. The arm-like appendage froze at an angle, giving them an opening out of the bedroom.

Her hands gripped the wrists of Canas, and the duo made a mad dash towards the door. While hurrying out of the room, the young boy managed to drop his flashlight; a companion used when reading stories underneath the covers on night's sleep evaded him-or when imagination was at its most pliable. The flashlight was also the only object he brought back from his journey in the Swiss Alps.

Back in the hallway, Chloi attempted to race towards the stairway, but terror seized her son. His body went limp and she fell to the floor, barely managing to cradle the fainted child. With no visible means of escape or protection she resorted to one final action, *prayer*. However, Chloi was too afraid to even know who or what she was praying to. A nameless chant escaped her lips while the air pressure intensified to the point where her bones crumbled into sediments.

Closing her eyes, with child tucked underneath her stomach, Chloi braced herself for the worst: would the arms burst through the door and impale her, maybe the touch could melt the membranes of her skin cells to the marrow, or maybe inhaling spores will eventually lead to tentacle sprouting from her skull?

Various colors flashed from underneath the door, vividly painting the hallway; if it were under safer circumstances, one would have even made a wish after gazing upon a wondrous sight. A blinding light appeared, stopping the prismatic rotation; above, she heard something that resembled a bomb detonating. Shortly after, a series of bangs discharged in the bedroom. And then, she was released from the burden of excessive gravity.

The lights, the putrid stench, the terrorizing grip of the being's presence was no longer tangible. Vanished. Canas finally stirred awake after a groan and a burp; Chloi opened the door to confirm her curiosity. The furniture was back upon the floor, slightly out of place, but still in a location like its original position. Everything was in order. However, sitting on the floor, where Canas had dropped his flashlight, was a slime covered book bag with a destroyed image of *the Caped Crusader*.

Frigicide

$\mathcal{B}$oreal gusts from the February blizzard thrashed against the rafters of a log cabin at the cliffside of a peak on the Appalachian Trail. Ice crept in through the gaps in the roof, depriving the interior of warmth. The cabin was erected in the late 19th century, utilizing the corpses of ancient evergreens to serve as foundation, and it received a necessary renovation within the last decade. Game hunters and seasoned hikers have taken shelter under this sturdy roof from the elements, or nocturnal scavengers. But tonight, this cabin's visitors were not hibernating. They were hiding.

The wooden door flung open, and two men tackled into the establishment. The first to rise, the one who led the rush, wore a bubble jacket with otter fur vestments, a wooly hat dusted in sleet, and rugged cargo pants. Hung around his thick neck was a pair of leather binoculars. He peered out the window, scanning the snowy landscape for anything other than cresting bands of snow. After leaving the frosted window, he slowly doused the oil lantern sitting on the floor. When he determined nothing to be present, the young man crouched next to the person laid out on the floor. "Alvin, you good? Are you alright?" he exhaled.

The younger brother clenched the zipper on his weatherproof parka and settled the bout of hyperventilation by pressing his back to the wall. "I'm fine. Yeah, I think I'm good. How are you, Oliver?" He nodded and his head flung droplets of snow to the floor. "What…what was that? It was in our tent…with us." He coughed, "did you get it? Attack it with your knife?"

"I think. It was moving so fast I couldn't tell."

"Was that *some bear*?"

"Too small to be a bear, and you saw. That thing didn't have any fur."

"But it had claws…tore through the whole camp. "

"I hope we never have to deal with it again," Oliver stated as he checked the door.

"What's that on your back?" Alvin weakly whispered.

The eldest quickly removed his coat: A large gash stretched from the shoulder to the coat tail, straight along the center of the spine. Edges of the lacerated tissue were caked with a black substance. "It smells like…sulfur," Alvin said.

The wind diminished as the ivory moon crept behind the peak of the ice-capped mountain range. As the commotion settled, Oliver stepped away from the window and joined his younger brother at the table. He rummaged through the satchel for any sort of rations and managed to salvage three protein bars. The rest of their belongings was at the base of the mountain, along with their camp, probably ransacked by whatever assaulted them in the dead of night. The bars were opened by Alvin, but Oliver turned his down.

"I shouldn't have brought you up here."

"Don't think like that," Alvin exhaled.

"No, I shouldn't. I should have waited until you were healthier before we did this."

"*We would never had made the climb if we waited til then*," he passively smiled. "I wanted us to go on this trip; we've talked about it for too long…the Appalachia."

"But I dragged you out here. Forced you to leave the comfort of your room."

"Hospice is far from comfortable; we don't even have streaming services." Alvin weakly laughed, then took his brother's firm fist into his hand. "Don't beat yourself up. We'll get through this, just like we always have."

Oliver replied. "Always the optimist, even when survival is at stake."

"When you've got stage-three thyroid cancer, survival is always at stake. Alvin checked out the rest of the cabin, "What do you think we should do? Send out a smoke SOS with the chimney? You're the expert on this."

"First, we should bar the door, in case it finds us. Whatever is out there will have a harder time getting through if we block it. Best bet is to wait until morning. Then we hike down, and call for help." Alvin bit his lip; he should've taken the phone out of the insulated tent before it was ripped to shreds.

"You think we'll be safe here? If that thing comes back…"

"It will have to find us, and if we keep a low profile, we should be safe."

"But this is an obvious hiding spot. Are you sure you want to lock us in?"

"Rather us be locked in here, than out in the subzero. The path is probably impossible to see. It'd be too dangerous for us to try and climb down the summit in the dark, and if we use light it might attract it…"

"Did you get a good look at *it*?" Alvin asked. The growls from his stomach indicated that he was behind on his meal schedule, and his medicine was back at base camp.

Specks of crystallized sweat bounced onto the blankets Oliver procured from the closet. "I could've seen anything in that snowstorm, but what I saw were wings, and teeth…" Alvin stopped toying with the oil lamp and glanced at his brother.

"*A predator.*"

"And we've been chosen as prey for whatever reason, but we won't go down like that. It's out there, so we should stay in here. At least until morning."

Oliver rose to his feet and began rearranging the furniture to barricade the entrance. He angled the hefty handcrafted dresser towards the door, tilted the circular wooden table to block the exposed windows, and broke the lantern to scatter shards of glass in front of each possible entrance. Propped in the corner, while gritting through the spasms happening in his chest, Alvin marveled at his brother's resourcefulness.

"This reminds me of old times," Alvin said holding his stomach.

"Oh…does it? How?"

"Remember how we used to hike out with dad? He and I would build snares for rabbits, and you'd try to pitch the tent by yourself but always end up giving up. We'd stay out till the sun went down, cook smores, name the clouds after our cartoon heroes; and, we played that one game. I forgot what it was called."

"A game?" Oliver chimed.

"Yeah, when we'd pretend to be animals and run wild. Let loose and be as primal as we wanted. You always wanted to be the wolf," he chuckled.

"Hm, the wolf is an intelligent creature."

"Even though you're not," Alvin teased, then sighed. "Those were the days, everything was so simple back then. Then, I went and got sick…" He broke eye contact with Oliver, and tickled a splintered beam hiding in the foundation. "Who would've thought that mom and dad passed the bad genes to me?"

"Don't blame them," Oliver comforted.

"I'm not. Nobody is to blame but myself, for being so weak," Alvin paused. A gale cut through the logs and stung their sullen eyes. "That's why you wanted to bring me up here, right? To show me I wasn't weak. So I could believe in my own strength? So I could learn to fight this disease instead of give up?"

"Guess you figured out my motive, huh?" Oliver nodded.

"My nurse told me your schemes. Nearly three months of planning and paperwork, I bet they required more signatures than the Constitution. Patients hardly leave."

"You're a special case. You're not some eighty-year-old geezer who can't care for his dentures."

"Yeah…but I'm still dying." Alvin reached for his side and massaged his laryngeal muscles, tenderly rubbing the swollen lump in his throat.

The repositioned furniture slightly creaked as the night progressed. More snow and ice pelted against the frozen windows. A groaning burp escaped the throat of the chimney; the brothers listened to echoes of the end of the world. In the stillness of the moonlight, an icicle broke from the roof and landed on the rafters. Both brothers perked like deer in headlights and waited for movement.

Nothing. But then…

"Did you hear that?" Alvin asked.

"No, what was it?"

"Sounded like a howl. Do you think it found us?"

"Doubtful," the eldest said.

"What about our tracks?"

"The blizzard probably covered them by now. Even ol Ham-bone and his bloodhound nose couldn't find us. And we put the lights out as soon as we came in."

"Right, you're right. I'm just on edge. I can't think straight in this cold!" Alvin shivered.

"You should get some rest then. We're hiking down the mountain at the first sign of light, and you'll need all the strength you can muster."

"Ha, just you wait. After this nap, I'll show you how strong I am."

"I most certainly do hope so." Oliver grinned from across the cabin before reaching for the cast iron prod in front of the fireplace.

ᴧᴧ

The band of flossed clouds slithered away from the silver moon, flooding the cabin with ivory light. As the beam crawled from one wall to the next, and across Alvin's eyes, it painted everything with a coat of peace. He awakened. After wiping the sleep from his face, he was met with a horrific sight.

A black humanoid laid directly next to him. The thing did not move, but it emitted an energy found in complex life forms, like humans. And then, the form pulled its chest apart, revealing a portal to a cosmic plane. Suddenly, a mighty vacuum dragged his body into the dimension, and devoured him with the formed darkness.

Alvin awoke in a cold sweat. A dream…?

He glanced at the phantom on the floor. Only his shadow, the projection of his sickly frame. Radiation had eaten away at much of his muscles, leaving a crackling skeleton in its wake. The youngest twirled his wrists, watching the darkness give form to his failing figure. His eyes eventually trailed from the extended fingers until they reached his sturdy boots.

Oliver peered through the silver window gripping the metal prod as if anticipating a brawl. The moon retracted behind a wave of snow, but before it tucked away, the younger brother failed to recognize his brother's shadow.

Or rather…his brother had no shadow at all. Along the floor were the shades of his boots, the iron in his hand, and even his hat; but, the direct body was absent in the projection.

"Hey, Oli-"

"Shhh," Oliver interrupted before placing his bony index finger over Alvin's lips. "Something is out there." Alvin cursed his body, the desire to throw up forced him to gag with a closed mouth. His gasps turned into tears and ballooned lungs.

Huff. Huff. Huff.

Trying to control his breathing, Alvin clasped his shaking hands together and tightened his fingers around each other.

Huff. Huff. Huff. Huff. Huff…

A growl came from outside the cabin and Alvin broke concentration. Knees contracted, giving him enough momentum to rise while using the wall as support. He nudged closer to the entrance, hoping to find his brother. As Alvin leaned against the sturdy board, the growl increased in volume;

whatever was outside was headed their way. "Oliver, where are you?" the youngest whispered once more to the shaded corners.

Footsteps shuffled along the boards. Suddenly, a frigid hand clasped against his shivering arm. He recognized the grooves of his brother's hand before they pulled him down. "It's...close," Oliver stated.

"I heard. What should we do?"

"Wait."

"Right, the entrances are blocked. There's no way it can come in."

"Exactly…" Oliver hacked a raspy cough. The growl outside suddenly changed into something more than a primal cry, it was a shout.

The room contained enough tension to melt the entire peak, and yet, the eldest was calm. His younger brother pressed his back against the wall once more and started to cry. "This is my fault. If I was stronger, we could leave. My damn body is failing me. I'm so useless!"

"Now's not the time."

"Now is exactly the time, because I know you, Oliver. You'll put yourself at risk for me, and...I can't have that."

"Alvin…" Oliver scuffed his beard.

"Remember that night when we promised not to abandon each other? It was the last venture we took with father before...before the diagnosis. That was the longest week of my life, I bet I slept a total of five hours. We only made it four point two miles into our four-month journey before I fainted from laryngeal complications. Instead of wandering in nature like we planned for half a year, I had two hospital visits, consults with three specialists, an MRI and a CT scan, a biopsy of the esophagus; and that was just the first day. You remember too, because you were there with me through all of it."

"Couldn't sleep either, those hospital chairs have no neck support."

"Their beds aren't much better. Anyways, that promise we made…the one at the start of the hike? You remember it?"

"Aye, we make it to the end…*together*."

"And we've lived up to that. You were there for me through all of this, and I helped you heal after those ugly college break ups," Alvin smirked-his brother was a doofus when it came to women.

"I honestly didn't think you could do it...but you proved me wrong. You're an oath keeper," Alvin tightened his lip, "which is why I'm taking back my word."

"This is not the time to be a martyr. Just stay cool, we can ride this thing out."

"No, we can't. I will stay here, and you..."

The shouting outside was barely audible, but it sounded strangely human. "If you leave, you can escape. I'm not going to be responsible for killing us both. I'm not afraid, Oliver. *I'm not afraid to die for you,* if it means saving you," Alvin adamantly stated.

The shouting outside transformed into words, and for a brief instant, the youngest believed he heard his name called amidst the whipping gusts.

"Ugh, it's that smell again. Sulfur..." Alvin whispered. "It found us. We're not safe anymore"

"*You were never safe.*" Oliver's grip tightened. Alvin tried to free his arm from the injurious grasp, but it wouldn't budge. "Oh...I can barely contain my appetite," he smacked his lips. The moon curled at the peak of its cycle, once more providing the cliff with light. The crystalized ice along the window panes refracted the beam, illuminating the cabin and the brothers. The youngest sat, horrified, as Oliver's shadow failed to produce again.

A loud bang cracked against the door. "Alvin! Alvin!"

He cocked his head like an alerted bird, "Who is that outside? And how do they know my name?"

"A bothersome pest...I should have thrown him off the cliff when I copied him; quite the fighter, I admit" Oliver muttered. "But he's too late, you've already invited me."

"What...what do you mean invited?" Alvin tried to hide the trembling hands underneath his parka, but his "brother" snatched them.

"*To the feast.*" Oliver let a baleful laugh expel before bringing the cancer-stricken hand to his mouth that gaped larger than a python's jaw.

The banging against the door continued until a piece of the furniture dislodged. "Open up! Alvin, it's me! Open up now!" the voice outside rang. He slammed through the entry, a serrated survival knife in his right hand. The sounds of a struggle happening in the far corner demanded his attention. Before Oliver dove into the fray, he caught sight of his younger brother weeping in the faint light. And...a second figure tearing its way through his parka.

"Get away now!" he shouted.

The phantom on the floor quickly released its vice grip as Oliver tackled it to the ground. The iron prod from the fireplace dropped. Retreating to the darkened corner, Alvin anxiously listened to the exchanging of blows.

A warm liquid splattered against his face, and the winter air congealed the blood. He gripped the metal rod; he wanted to help his brother. But, at this moment, he wasn't sure which one was the real Oliver. Would he randomly strike in the dark injuring them both, or would he wait until one was on the verge of being beaten, and then strike the other?

The noises of the scuffle slowly dissipated as the sound of a knife being extracted from flesh cut the howling wind. Both bodies were tossed onto the floor, yet only one of them moved. Alvin held tight to the bar, still unsure on what choice to make. The moonlight peered through the window and revealed Oliver's bloody face. His eyes were feral from the fight, and they glazed as if he were going to pounce on Alvin and tear him limb from limb.

"*I made a promise,*" Oliver's cracked lips curled.

"What the hell? No, no, this is too much. How do I know it's you? Like it's really you?" Alvin interrogated.

"I'm still covered in snow," Oliver said.

Alvin dropped the rod to the side and embraced his savior.

"That thing…it looked just like you. Ah hell, how? How? HOW?! "

"Disgusting," Oliver panted. "Whatever it is, it's dead now."

"I was in here…with it, the whole time."

"Did you not recognize it wasn't me?"

"No," Alvin stiffened. "I couldn't tell; it mimicked you perfectly. Talked like you, walked like you...and it even had *your memories.* That's...I'm not sure what to believe."

Oliver surveyed the damaged cabin. He propped the table back on its side and noticed the shards of glass both in his palm and on the floor. "That's a lot of blood. Where'd the glass come from?" he then tore a section of his tattered shirt and wrapped the wound.

"The lantern," Alvin nodded. "He…it…broke it when we first entered. I can't make sense of any of this. Oliver! It was you! Like you, undeniably. How can this have happened? There are some things science still can't explain. Like my sickness...and now this."

"Science may not have an answer, but superstitions are always out there."

"Do you know something?" Alvin coughed.

"The only thing I can think of is a story a few hiking buddies of mine used to share when we camped out in the Blue Ridge. Used to hit the Appalachian when the leaves changed colors, a marvelous sight from the summit. At night we'd sit out by the fire, pounding back beers and curing jerky; sharing stories too."

"What did they say?"

"Usually land untouched by civilization has legends from the indigenous residents, but there are no historical accounts of this. No tribal myths or tall tales." The knife was stained with red blood, and the smell of iron filled the claustrophobic cabin. "Only within the last twenty or so years have hikers begun experiencing savage attacks on these trails."

Oliver laid his bleeding palm onto the table and stared at his brother. "I don't know much; sightings only happen in high altitudes. Some say they're rogue angels who come down and possess people; others believe them to be akin to drifting spirits."

"Angels? Attacking humans? That's crazy, even by my standards." Alvin coughed a wad of phlegm of blood on the floor, his breathing was shallow and full of liquid. The eldest pushed the dresser out of the way to allow light to sink into the cabin. Laying on the floor was the homunculus wrapped in Oliver's parka. Fur from his jacket meshed with the edges of the wound, the white tufts soaked in crimson.

"Not attack. *Eat.*"

"It did mention a feast. So…evil angels, they come and eat people. What are they called?"

"The Arix. Allegedly, they initially appear in dreams."

"Where do they come from? Are they rare, or many?"

"Ha you're really taken with this, but I'm glad you are. That's survival. Out here in the wilderness, you must assume *everything is real*, even if it's not."

"Even if it's not..." Alvin shuttered. "What now?"

"We head back down," Oliver threw his arm over his shoulder to support his younger brother. "I'd rather not stay here and wait to see what happens to this thing." He slammed the toe of his boot into gut of the faceless humanoid before throwing his brother over the shoulder and departing from the cabin.

^^

A fresh layer of snow blanketed of the cliffside, but Oliver was able to locate the tracks from his hasty ascent. "This way," he said as they embarked down, hobbling like a three-legged beast of burden.

"How can you see anything?"

Oliver smiled, "We'll let the moon guide our path. The clouds are pretty thick, but we'll go steady, so we don't step over any edges."

"I'll pass on that. Death by plummeting off a mountainside is a fate worse than cancer." Alvin's breath was thin and labored. The two continued their descent, shuffling slowly. The howling wind hushed, and the flakes gently rolled to the snowy blanket. Atop the summit the musing of the modern world seemed insignificant, underwhelming compared to the sheer magnificence of the winter horizon, the ice capped peaks clawing for heaven as the scattered stars heightened the sublime scenery only experienced here, where man has yet to invade, where the trees and elements of nature rule supreme.

"How many nights by the watering hole did we spend just aimlessly staring at the stars?" Oliver asked.

"I did most of the staring; you used to make out with Erin Lancaster."

He chuckled, "Wonder whatever happened to her? She had the softest lips, even though her breath smelled like honeydew all the time. You know, when we make it off this mountain, I'll give her a call."

"You don't think she has a family by now? That was almost fifteen years ago."

"Won't know until I call," he laughed. "Maybe fifteen years is enough time for her to come back around. Hopefully, I can get Ma and Pops off my back about grandkids. They keep pestering me."

"No surprise there, I know they don't expect me to carry on the family legacy, so the pressure falls to you. But you're the oldest, so it's always been on you."

Oliver glanced skyward, "I always knew it, I just tried to avoid thinking about it. I tend to have that habit."

An hour or so passed and the two finally reached the tree line. The tundra met the forest but all the trees, aside from the coniferous evergreens were stripped bare. Black and iced bark vigilantly kept watch on the world.

"Are we headed back to base camp?" Alvin inquired while briskly rubbing his hands together for warmth.

"Nah, straight to the bottom. Moon's coming back out, we should pick up our pace. We can salvage our gear later; our top priority is safety. And a glass of bourbon when we get to the closest settlement." He provided his sickly brother with a crutch, the snow melted underneath the weight of their insulated boots.

"Strange, we haven't seen any other hikers. I thought you said this was a popular summit."

Oliver processed his response before sharing, "It is...I usually run into a handful or so each time I hike this peak."

"Do you think the Arix...could've gotten them?" Alvin shuddered.

"Doubtful. It's the off-season, so most trails are naturally vacant."

"And if that isn't the reason? If they were...attacked? Like us?"

"Then we pray for those lost. But, at least the thing is dead now."

"Not exactly, because if someone checks that cabin, they aren't going to find a monster. *They are going to find you.*" The dead figure was, indeed, shaped exactly in his likeness. "Someone is going to report you as deceased."

"Let them, at least I gave my life for someone I love: *You.* Now I have to start over as something new but that's alright." Alvin cackled at his brother's humor, but his grin contorted into a sinister leer.

As they wandered through the frozen trees, an iced branch above them broke from the weight of the deposits of snow. Oliver pushed his brother away, taking the brunt of the crash. The object fell from a height of eighteen feet and slammed right into his shoulder. "Ahhhh! That went straight for the bone" he howled.

He tried to rise to his feet but the jolting pain from his arm caused temporary paralysis. The frosted rime bit his legs and cut his nerves. Oliver checked his shoulder. Dislocated.

He brought the tuft of his hood into his mouth and firmly gripped the dislocated arm. With all his might, Oliver jammed the ball back into its socket and pain erupted from his arm like an exploding super volcano. The site would need treatment once they arrived at the base...but a fear gripped Oliver: What if only one of them made it, or worse...*neither*?

The searing pain from his immobile shoulder heightened his sense of caution. As he rose, utilizing the same branch that fell, he noticed a fresh trail of prints in the snow. Kneeling next to the disturbance, he also realized that his brother was surprisingly quiet. Next to a set of boot heels were claw marks. Roughly a foot in length with five defined digits, each bearing a serrated tip. He didn't have time to speculate what could've attacked but he was aware of what laid in the cabin, and that his brother was in danger.

Oliver followed the prints and immediately began shouting for Alvin. "I should've thrown that thing over the cliff." He shouted again but only heard the frozen branches scratching against the bark. With no choice but to follow the path, for the sake of his sibling, Oliver progressed into the tundra wielding the branch as a walking cane.

Or a weapon, if needed.

The forest condensed the farther down he went, and the moon faintly peered through the dense thicket. After a few failed attempts at call-and-response, Oliver threw himself against an evergreen, the slush chilling his spine. His voice was raw from screaming in the subzero temperatures.

Far off in the darkness, a branch cracked, and then another, and another.

Oliver scanned the area and confirmed his suspicions when he saw a highlighter orange band gently fluttering from a dead branch: their tent. The refuge that housed their bodies only hours before the savage attack.

An opening between the trees allowed enough light to peer down on his position, and Oliver dropped his stick. Standing in front of the tent, with his arm extended like a welcoming usher was Alvin. In his hand was the special bottle of craft bourbon Oliver packed-he originally wanted to celebrate their lives with a hearty toast on the mountaintop.

Strangely, his brother was standing tall, taller than he'd ever seen the cancer patient stand before; and there was an ephemeral glow radiating from his skin as if he'd received a transfusion of blood containing photons. Alvin then removed his overcoat as well as the rest of his clothing-much to his brother's protesting. Oliver pressed forward to stop him until the moon bathed the clearing. His eyes trailed from the remains of their campsite to his brother's shadow.

Or at least where it should've been.

The stretch of tundra was empty, no trace of the shadow cast behind him. Oliver tightened his hold on the branch but dropped it after witnessing the next sight.

"Now, humor me. What was that game you used to play? Ah, that's right. Morphin…" Alvin wrapped his arms around his back, bent at the hips and pulled from the spine. Flaps of warm flesh oozed as they peeled away from the sickly skeleton, exposing the vertebral column. From the moist cadaver jutted four appendages at ninety-degree angles-the symmetry between either side was so precise it was considered sacred. Oliver gasped in horror as the wings beat thrice to cleanse the gore of the body. The upper two wings were covered in misty white feathers that glistened like the flakes falling from heaven; the lower leathery like the wings of a demonic bat.

"What…what the hell?" a terrified Oliver shouted.

"You're well informed, for a human." The thing spoke but Alvin's mouth did not move, rather, the leathery wings flapped.

"No…"

"You guessed it: Arix. However, we don't like the term *angel*; they are passive-aggressive pushovers."

With adrenaline coursing through his veins, Oliver reached for the stick, and swung with all his might; but it passed through Alvin as if he'd swung at mist.

"You can stop now, it's inevitable," the creature lulled with its leathery wings. Ignoring his request, Oliver continued to thrash the apparition until the radiating pain in his shoulder forced him to drop the branch. "You've got spunk. Nobody tries to fight back anymore," the Arix whispered. Its voice soothing like somber waves crashing against a rocky shore. "I couldn't even possess you completely; only had time to mimic your image before you woke. Most don't even realize I'm present until it's too late, not you nor your brother.

"What did you do with my brother!?" he screamed.

The Arix dipped behind the tree and smiled; his teeth coated with bubbling sulfur. "First, can I say, what a fantastic relationship you two have. Your brother, Alvin, *he loved you*, there's no doubt. I wandered all through his mind while you carried this copy down the mountain. He's had a few rough years lately? Eaten away by cancer, a financial burden to your parents, even forced you to withdraw from university to cover cost. I'd say your brother is resting peacefully but lying is not my strong suit. You should know though, even when he was sick, he tried his best to live up to your standards.

"Isn't that why you brought him here, Oliver? To test his strength...no, that wasn't it. Not for him at least. You came up here for that, but he came...he came to say goodbye."

"Shut up, don't you dare talk about my brother! Tell me, where is Alvin!?"

"That's a difficult question to answer," the Arix snickered. It clapped once, and the creature levitated, hovering a foot above the ground despite the wings remaining immobile.

"Technically he's here," the creature tapped its head. "But…he's also in the Void. There won't be any coming back for him."

Oliver stared deep into its eyes before frigid tears swept down his frostbitten cheeks. "As for what happened to him…well, I'm sure you can figure that out."

Oliver dropped to his knees, snow rubbing against his thick pants. The Arix knelt beside him with a devilish grin, the four wings vibrating at sonic speed.

"How is this happening?"

"*You invited me.*"

"What…do you mean?" Alvin whimpered.

"We are bound by an oath; in exchange for a cosmic palate, we are not allowed to feast on sentient beings...unless they grant us an invitation to do so."

"I never invited you."

"But you claimed you were willing to accept death on my behalf. That is consent. '*At least I gave my life for someone I love?*' Realize, there are loopholes to every law" The creature's tone fluctuated, and for a brief second, he heard his brother's voice. "A joke to you, but that's a meal ticket for me," the Arix crooned with the black wings.

"Then…" Oliver broke down.

"Your brother, Alvin, invited me in the cabin. He put his life at stake, for the sake of saving you. Quite touching. But he was too frail to provide nourishment. Somber memories are tasteless, I prefer the memories of the single-minded," the Arix picked its teeth with a plucked feather.

"The true delicacy your race is that crispy conscious stored in that little cerebrum. Carbon is too heavy of an element to digest, so we only savor the serotonin and hormones." The Arix then expanded its wings, stretching eight-feet in each direction. "That cognition cocktail can drive a devil crazy;

and it's impossible to get that flavor in the **Void**." A banshee-like scream howled throughout the wilderness, echoing all the way to the abandoned cabin.

"Alvin...Alvin...I'm so sorry," Oliver pounded his chest.

He didn't need to know how this story ended; it would end the same way it did for all the other hikers who met their demise on the mountaintop: in snow and blood. "Before you...do whatever it is you're going to do, make me a promise. An oath."

"Dealing with the devil?" the creature beat its bottom wings. "Why not? What is it?"

"Don't impersonate him anymore, please. Let Alvin rest in peace. If you need a host...*use me*. Just let my brother rest, he deserves it." The Arix stared deeply into the blank eyes of Oliver, before beating its wings against the incoming gale.

"Deal," its forked tongue slithered. "I must warn you though, you will be unable to find peace so long as I remain you. Another law..."

"No loopholes for that one, huh?" Oliver grunted.

The Arix howled again before simultaneously clapping its hands and wings. With the force of a hurricane, the creature blasted into the sky, breaking the snow, branches, rocks, and legs of Oliver. Thrown yards away on his back, the surviving sibling closed his eyes in acceptance. In the darkness of imagination, he attempted to replay his life in these final moments, cherishing snapshots soon to be savored by this galactic gourmand.

However, he was only able to remember a sole scene from his childhood: A lazy summer sunset spent at the pond concealed by the Blue Ridge mountains; the scent of cut pine blending with pollen; the murky water enveloping Alvin's robust body as he cannonballed from the cliff; and, the taste of honeydew embedded in Erin Lancaster's soft lips.

Gangrene

Grand Wizard Roth, I fear that we've committed *a grave sin*," a feminine voice cries through a headset connected to a sixteen-inch personal laptop.

"Servant of almighty Saturn, explain. What has you wretched in agony?" A pudgy, middle-aged man wearing black eyeliner appears in the web cam chat room. The feedback from the surround sound rings through Roth's office, which is coincidentally his bedroom.

Expansive textbooks with enlarged Latin symbols cover the table, and empty picture frames hang along the chipped walls; cast on the damp floorboards are robes moist with sweat. Arranged in a heptagon, on the desk, are thirteen black candles, many of them exposing a charred wick. The room stinks of unbathed bodies, rotting roots, and mercury-one of the more toxic ingredient used in necromantic rituals.

A window pops up on the corner of Roth's monitor: INCOMING CALL. "Your partner is on the other line. He wants to merge calls." The Grand Wizard double-taps ACCEPT, and the three-way video chat connects.

"He's calling you? He shouldn't be..."

Her face contorts; suddenly, Roth wonders if an error was made by allowing his apprentice to enter their conversation. The sight on the screen confirms his suspicions.

Malach. The normally robust, mid-twenties man is a skeleton; anemic, suffering from severe weight loss, and his skin is scattered with mustard yellow patches. He draws a guttural breath, "Roth."

"My dutiful apprentice, what has happened to you? Why...do you look-"

"Malach! What have you done?" the woman shouts. "Why are you still in your apartment? You've got to hide. The police came looking for you."

"I will not be here long."

"Malach, please..." she begs.

The enigmatic Malach gurgles in his microphone, his rancid breath fogs the lens. "As for what I have done...well, I did what any magician would do: *I casted a spell*. But Grand Wizard, if I'm not mistaken, this is your first introduction to my Septum, Bezel. She is somewhat new to our craft but shows great potential."

Bezel's facial features are plain-cheeks free of any foundation or blush. Brown eyes, wide and inquisitive like those with limitless imagination; yet there's a depth to the pupils darkened by the shade of impending doom.

The Grand Wizard scratches the arch of his curly eyebrow, "Bezel, was it? No, we are not personally acquainted, but I am curious as to why you contacted me and not Malach. Is that not one of our communication clauses? Perhaps he can dispel this confusion…"

"I contacted you because we are in a dire situation," she releases an exhaustive sigh.

"Malach, why should I believe her?"

"She has been instrumental in my recent endeavors. Two completed seances, the conjuring of familiars-both corporeal and ectoplasmic-there is even footage of her summoning a succubus to perform…certain services for us."

"A worthy apprentice for you, the Midwestern magician of macabre. Your ambition has carried our teachings to new realms; now the entire world can bear witness to our dark arts."

"Your praises are welcomed, but thin. I did not study magic to gain titles," he curtly remarks to Roth. Malach adjusts the black device, changing the angle of the webcam. His fingernails are gnawed and severely inflamed, and his wrist thin to the point that his veins can be traced by a pencil. "My liege, my teacher, I must confess."

"What troubles you?" Roth raises the brightness on his computer display.

"I have been chosen. Almighty Saturn has chosen me to usher in a new epoch and with their blessing I have accomplished a feat that none in this age have attempted; the spell we conjured will reshape the nature of the world, erecting a new pillar of society with necromancy etched at its peak. However, there is no room for false prophets in this dynasty."

"*You succeeded…?*" Bezel murmurs.

The Grand Wizard turns his attention to Bezel's screen, "What is this spell? And why have you yet to tell me anything?"

"My apologies. I…I am still shaken to see Malach on the other line. He's jeopardizing his safety by conversing with us. However, I digress." Bezel shifts gears, "Grand Wizard, have you watched the news today?"

"No, I have abstained from television," he confesses.

"Well, the local stations are abuzz with a story. They are presenting facts alternative to the truth-not necessarily false information, but rather presented from a perspective intent to spin a dramatic narrative. However, only by my version will you be able to understand what has befallen us.

Malach...do you wish to share it?" He declines the opportunity with a delayed shake of his head. Wearily, Bezel repositions the desktop chair. A burdened breath departs her lips, "Grand Wizard Roth, it all started with a *tome*."

Ein

I am aware that most tales of the macabre begin in the bellows of a thundering storm; however, this story starts underneath the Midwestern sun in the town of Lindsborg, Kansas. Fall was evident everywhere one turned: the color of the leaves had transformed from green to orange, amber, hazel, and goldenrod. Diesel tractors hummed while lands lay bare now that crops were harvested. Main Street was decorated with turkey feathers and images of pasty-faced pilgrims; Thanksgiving was but a week away, and the entire town was preparing for the fellowship and feast. With a population of less than three thousand, Lindsborg had the essentials of a small town in the Rust Belt. Streets were lined with old warehouses and factories, the relics of the steel industry. There was only one of each civic institution: police station, library, hospital (the only building with four floors), and a city hall that played ragtime music at 5 P.M. We were lucky enough to have a movie theater, which I frequented often.

Although most Lindsborg foundations were abandoned and eroded to rust, the townsfolk were the source of life. This is a town where smiles and waves were exchanged upon passing, and the churches-and Golden Corral-are always packed on Sundays. Nearly every family has been here for at least four generations and were well acquainted with each other. Except us. But we proudly adopted our titles as outcasts from their sappy society.

Now, I am a native of Kansas, hailing from the outskirts of Wichita, born to a wheat and corn farming family. Being the daughter of farm hands, I was blessed with uncanny strength and vigor-my mother often commended on the passion of my spirit. The agricultural lifestyle is mentally exhausting, despite the simplicity of it. One must remember everything from the harvest moon to the necessary distance between planted seeds, the rain and dry seasons-that happen all too often in the Midwest-how to combat the migratory insects when they stop for a snack, the signs of an infected crop that required immediate extermination. But I managed to adapt to the work, and with a renowned joy. Although quite handy with the hoe, I was not a stellar student. After graduating with one cord (still unsure how I earned it), I performed various odd jobs and peculiar tasks in order to help my family with their stacking bills; this monotonous routine continued until I met Malach this previous summer.

I'm sure that you are familiar with your apprentice's past, but for the sake of this story allow me to grace your ears-it may also provide context to our current situation. He was conceived to be a drifter; born to couple who traveled across the nation with a circus troupe. His mother died during a botched C-section; some blame the surgeon who completed the delivery, for he'd been diagnosed with psoriatic arthritis. This sudden hardship left Jeremy Thomas in a tight bind while he raised the boy who would become Malach.

An entertainer of little fame in the circus industry, Jeremy mostly worked the ticketing booth; but, rumors state that his rare shows were the most aberrant out of the entire carnival. Perhaps that is due to his inclusion of young Malach in his inexplicable performances, which some say included rope bindings, hypnotic dances and ritualistic chanting, and the skin of wild critters.

The generations changed, and as people became socially conscious, less individuals visited *the freakshow*; this prompted eventual termination of the cross-country carnival, as well as the careers it offered. Malach and his illiterate father were forced to settle in the town of Lindsborg, Kansas.

Lacking any real education, save for the skills he learned while on the road, his father had great difficulty finding a stable job that didn't involve gruesome manual labor, pushing them to the brink of poverty. This streak was broken when one day, by fate or luck (whichever is your preference), his Jeremy was hired.

The profession? *Caretaker for the county morgue.*

Since Malach was nurtured by the bizarre circus acts, and had no interaction with the public-school system, his natural assignment was to his single father. Together, their days were spent embalming the recently deceased, stuffing ashes into elaborate vases, dressing the corpses for the wake, all while maintaining the integrity of the morgue. Malach was not allowed to directly handle the bodies, for he was a minor, but he was a devoted assistant to his father's craft.

The duo made enough money to rent a one-story townhome not too far from the main street of Lindsborg. Jeremy occasionally performed in neighboring towns, which earned bonus cash; and with it he was able to make an important purchase that shaped Malach into the man he is today: a Macintosh computer with internet access.

However, tragedy struck before Jeremy was able to use it. He became ill by contracting a resistant strain of tuberculosis from a woman who recently died while in the bustling city of New York. The city officials permitted Malach to take over as the morgue caretaker since he'd been trained (and so few could stomach the profession).

I am uncertain exactly when Malach decided to give his soul to the eternal abyss, but he mentioned the decision was based on the failing health of his sole parent. For months, he watched his sickly father toil with the dead, skin bleached due to his lungs blooming with tuberculosis. While he cared for him at home (they had no health insurance, and no hospital would accept a live strain of TB), Malach preoccupied himself with the computer. That device became his portal to a limitless world, and without parental control, his view was unfiltered. Eventually, he stumbled upon a video recording of a Grand Wizard performing a three-hour divination involving a dead tree and two snakes with sapphire scales. His interest was piqued, and appetite whet for an understanding of the arcane craft. From that point he dedicated himself to practicing the dark arts, perhaps in hopes to save his father.

But on Malach's nineteenth birthday, Jeremy Thomas drew his final breath. As if fate weren't cruel enough, Malach was tasked with cleaning the body. After the records were taken, he decided to have his father cremated-a funeral was too expensive. Since that birthday, Malach became a servant of Saturn, furiously perfecting the craft of necromancy in hopes to become a Grand Wizard. It would be another four years before our paths crossed in the most unusual of circumstances.

That summer, I managed to pick up a new position of employment that fit my lifestyle. I'd only begun dabbling in necromancy when I was hired at Crown & Roots, the local apothecary. As the new clerk in the herbal shop (the only shop for twenty miles), my task was to have complete knowledge of the inventory, and how to grow or procure it. On that fateful day, I was tending to some freshly picked rosemary when he entered the store.

Upon our initial introduction, I would have never guessed that this customer was an apprentice of the arcane, for he wore navy jeans, a plain black t-shirt, and his face was free from any tattoos or piercings; one would even consider him somewhat handsome. His head was shaped like an arrow jutting into tomorrow, but he slouched his shoulders often eliminating the confidence that may have been present. We exchanged the usual customer/clerk banter until it came time for him to purchase the items on his list. I immediately recognized the peculiarity of the objects requested-for they lacked practical or culinary use. The items included wormwood, frog's breath, nightshade, a clove of purple garlic, lamb's ear, and the petals of a black dahlia. At the time, I was still scratching the surface of the dark arts, but I was informed enough to engage him in conversation regarding the black dahlia-it is an ideal offering to a departed soul. He was impressed by my knowledge, and then divulged his plans, which fascinated me for various reasons.

How refreshing it had been to meet another magician; for too long I believed myself to be the only seer within this backwater state. Our companionship was instant, and the two of us spent the entirety of the summer performing rituals and recording them to be uploaded to the internet. Malach was no stranger to the occult and willing to entreat the ephemeral in pursuit of empowerment. I considered him a pioneer, unafraid to conjure creations from the netherworld for the simple sake of growth.

Thus began our journey as neo-necromancers.

I

After successfully completing the conjuring of a bat familiar on Sunday, Malach and I decided to return to his residence and recharge our energies. For the past month we toiled to perform this spell; under the waxing moon of the previous night, our combined efforts were rewarded. The fresh remains of the bat reanimated and took flight.

Astounded, I watched the impossible become real, however, in my partner I recognized a restless anxiety. Honestly, these assigned rituals were considered amateur regarding astral arts. Malach had years of experience over me, yet he was tasked with the apprentice-level spells to perform. He'd wanted to expand his necromantic arts and begin the Abysmal Trials-the nightmarish ordeal required to become a Grand Wizard-but he had little chance to practice. Knowing this, I could only stay so excited as the leathery wings of the bat finally stopped beating and the corpse crashed against the soaked earth.

We reached Malach's studio apartment and were surprised to find a young boy sitting at the doorstep. Looking no older than eight, the boy wore a magnificent garb: jewels aligned his puffed shoulders, mushroom-colored boots polished in the light, and his white pants were neatly tailored to fit his frame. But what I remember most vividly was the shape of his pupils, they engulfed the entirety of the young boy's eyes. How *black* they were…darker than any shade of midnight that I'd witnessed in my twenty-four years of life.

To distract himself, the boy was poking at something black and formless with a stick. As we approached him our natural human instincts arose. I tried to locate a parent in the surrounding area; but, before either of us could address the lost child, we were halted by the horrendous sight. The object that he'd been poking on the ground was a *bloated rat.* Maggots and gram-negative bacteria had eaten through the creature's flesh, giving unsuspecting residents of the complex an uncomfortable view of its spoiled innards. And the boy's, I dare say, joyful stabbing of the deceased beast made the cold run through my bones.

There was something sinister about the young child. His presence alone intensified the pulsing of my veins, and my vision became hypersensitive, turning the sublime sunset into a kaleidoscope of terror. As we neared him, I caught sight of a box sitting next to him. A package roughly the size of a small cabinet drawer. It was made from cardboard, yet it was soggy and wrapped in ten-gallon trash bags. There were recent reports that orphans had been seeking homes but judging by his attire I knew the boy had not come to seek refuge.

The enigmatic child cocked his head to the side and greeted me with an ivory smile; his perfectly defined teeth cut through the afternoon haze.

Malach was the first to approach him, for it was his apartment. "You need to get into the apartment kid? Lost? Or just waiting on someone?"

The child cocked his head toward Malach with inhuman speed. He stared at my partner intensely, and then shot a leer in my direction. He lifted the medium-sized package off the sidewalk, placing it in his hands. "Yes, I have been waiting for you. This is *your father's last will.*" The delivery boy giggled and sprinted away into an alley; before either of us could give chase a bulb of thunder exploded nearby. It immobilized the both of us and instinctively we tried to cover our ears. The ringing subsided after a couple of seconds and we immediately investigated the corner the child had turned. But to our surprise we were met with nothing out of the ordinary, except a shimmering globule dripping from one of the industrial trash can. The boy was gone. Yet, I've failed to remove that grin from my memory, nor the maggots engorging on the dead rat with a stick impaled in the swollen stomach.

Upon entering the apartment, the first thing Malach did was unwrap the package. Although he rarely discussed it, Malach had a disagreement with his dad the night before his nineteenth birthday, before Jeremy died. I assumed this to be part of his driving force for power; the loss of a family member can make one resort to *extreme* measures. He tore through the cardboard while I contemplated the origins of the delivery boy. His late father had worked in the circus business, and it was true that there were freaks among men (depending on how one defines man); but this boy was no carny. He lacked any desire to entertain.

How long had he been waiting here for us anyways?

Scraps of the package were thrown across the furnished apartment and Malach beckoned me to join him at the brown dining room table. We pushed the circular placemats to the side, making room for the object that had been gifted to us, and together prepared to uncover this mystery. What exactly had Malach's father bequeathed to him?

A grimoire, or a tome. The binding was wrapped in a splotchy, self-lubricating substance, giving it the appearance of lungs excised from a chronic smoker. The edges were lined with objects that resembled human incisors. As Malach opened the ghastly tome, a foul stench came out from the pages. Typically, his apartment smelled of fried bacon, scented candles, and herbs; that was replaced by the putrid odor of a peat bog. A flaccid maggot crawled out from underneath the book onto the table and I quickly swatted it away; it was customary for old texts to house insect eggs, especially if they'd been in storage. My insides lurched at the sight-although I dabble in necromancy, I was never a fan of the bulging grubs.

On the inside of the cover were two feathers, bound at the quills, with a congealed liquid caking the tip. Being well-versed in alchemical ingredients, I immediately recognized the shimmering pinions: feathers from the sacred Pharaoh vulture. Never have I heard of a ritual that required the use of such a prized item. Some necromancers go their entire life without ever laying eyes upon one; and, here we were, with *two* in our possession. Next to the feathers was a rectangular case that contained a cast-iron needle; there was also a silver ring with a gray jewel in the hilt.

I inspected the peculiar contents; Malach hurriedly flipped through the pages, until he tapped "the teeth" on the back cover.

"The pages are blank. *All of them.*"

At first, I didn't believe him, maybe he'd not gone far enough, but for the next two minutes we combed through the thousand-page volume unable to find a visible trace of ink. Upon this realization, my head spun, and frustration overtook me. Were we being had by someone? Why four years after his father's death had this "last will" suddenly appeared? More importantly, who possessed it until this point?

Fatigued from the day, and secretly wanting to celebrate the completion of our hexing ritual, I called for Malach to close the book and join me on the couch to watch the latest episode of our guilty pleasure: *Chicago Fire* However, before our show began, the nine o'clock news had five more minutes of airtime.

The stories of the town continued to pour into our apartment: a cotton-haired teacher was awarded the "Lifetime Leader Award" for fifty years of work, a supporter of the current tyrant of a president commented on his claims of fraudulent statements, the Lindsborg Lions softball team was en route Topeka to compete in the state championships tournament for the second year in a row.

As we decompressed, and caught wind of the daily musings, I noticed the fracture in my partner's countenance-his anxiety was flaring. The morgue was set to receive an upgrade and Malach, being the obedient worker he is, decided to spearhead the project. However, it eventually turned into him being the sole member of the renovation committee. The state department also demanded outlandish upgrades and weren't willing to inch on the projected budget. Surely, anybody would be stressed, but imagine having to share that frustration with only formaldehyde corpses. Now, we'd been pranked by receiving this useless book. These worries quickly dissipated when an alert notification pulsed on the television.

II

While I still lived in Wichita, I played on every sports team my high school offered; I was quite the athlete-my mother says the strongest women are rooted in soil. Being the small town that it is, Lindsborg only had one high school, and our school would often play against them. We met the same girls on the athletic fields as we grew up, establishing somewhat of a friendly rivalry with their players. Their soccer and basketball teams were sub-par; however, when it came to softball, the Lindsborg Lions were undefeated. And it was thanks to one player: *Miranda Marshalls*.

At fifteen, she was the star pitcher of the varsity team as a freshman, and even threw her first no-hit game (of nine that season) on her debut appearance. Her team won the state championship, three years in a row. A regular home run hitter, her batting average was a .396 over the four seasons she played. But her life off the field was equally impressive; weekends were spent at the soup kitchen, and, after softball practice she tutored middle-schoolers in arithmetic.

Although she was quite the star student-and star athlete-Miranda was a *repulsive* sight. Large bodied, with the face of a Viking, her size made her tower over most of the football team, and her skin constantly shed. Situated on her asymmetrical face was a bulbous nose, flaky and chapped lips, and her upper maxilla contained an extra snaggletooth.

The last time we met was on the softball field, at least five years ago. Does one ever reminisce on the rudeness of youth? Because there is an inherent evil within it. It began with some of Lindsborg Lions teasing their star pitcher about prom. One girl, I believe her name was Nancy Cotton, went as far as to play a prank upon the unsuspecting victim earlier at their school. Rumors reached our locker room before we readied to play: apparently, one of the basketball players pretended to ask Miranda to prom only to publicly humiliate her by making out with Nancy at the lockers (a common farce). The school day ended with Miranda running out of her trigonometry quiz, with tears in her swollen eyes, and Nancy sitting in her chair with a devious smile.

However, in the sixth inning of our game, Miranda shifted on the pitcher's mound, and threw the ball with such devilish fury towards the unsuspecting bully guarding second base. Four of Nancy ribs cracked when the baseball embedded into her chest. I still remember the sound of the bones snapping; a tightening, spine-tingling noise that one never forgets. The poor girl was escorted off the field, and Miranda was benched for the rest of the game. Witnessing such an act frightened me, yet, set me on my path to owning my true self. Here was a girl, the same age as me, using violence to attain healing; you must realize this was unheard of in Kansas.

The news report stated Marshalls failed to show up at the community center-to help facilitate bingo this past Friday. A few dutiful citizens became worried, and reported the girl missing after she did not come the next morning-for pickleball. It was highly unlike her to skip out on a shift, and the times she did not show, she always called beforehand with a viable explanation. To go missing in a small town will always cause a stir, and lead to the collective distrusting each other, but her absence was the beginning of something much worse.

Horace Martin, a retired Vietnam vet who tended the grounds of the old Kanerbort Steel Mill, was cutting the grass around the tool shed when he noticed one of the doors leading to the main warehouse was cracked. Holding this position for nearly thirty years, the elephant-skinned man knew this place better than his own home, which some say was covered with empty shell casings and bottles. He decided to check out the occurrence; convinced that he'd properly locked up the last time he entered the mill, which was nearly three days prior. While inspecting the expansive, bleak warehouse, he came across two sets of footprints in the dust below, and a few of the instruments were out of position; most notably, a hammer was missing from the rack of tools. Utilizing his military training, Horace tracked the set of footprints to a rusted standalone locker, entered the combination, and swung open the door…

"Violent death," Malach stated. "Hammer to the back of the head, body broken and discarded in a locker, clothes still worn." The word DEAD was plastered under her portrait, a low-quality shot of Miranda wearing the Lindsborg Lions softball jersey. *Her spirit may never leave that mill*," he shuddered.

"That's crazy, I knew her. Kind of." I uttered loud enough for Malach to break out of his shell. Sweat rolled down my friend's salt-white skin as if he was wrestling with a bout of hysteria. He stayed silent but continued to focus on the information recited by the news anchor. I went back to the report with even more inquisitiveness; death has a strange way of making us revisit the past. Suddenly, I wanted to learn more about Miranda, who'd I only knew through our chance meetings on the field.

The news report ended, and soon the introduction to our show started, but I decided to mute the television. I cracked open the bottle of whiskey purchased on the way home. The celebration had been postponed long enough. What were we celebrating again?

A successful binding of a spirit to the body.

Now, to one who is unacquainted with conjuration of familiars, they may not understand the difficulty of this act. To contact a being beyond the Schism is an elaborate feat, even a low-class entity expends an immense amount of energy. To bind a soul, one requires the obvious: a soul, and a host. But there are additional ingredients that are required (runes and alchemical potions to enhance the spell's potency). A series of conditions must be fulfilled-precisely, I might add. An ideal location must be secure; it must behave as a conduit for astral energies. All this must be done before the actual ritual can begin, which, is an arduous process; lasting typically hours or days, and some of the higher-level arts have been known to require a fortnight. If only it were as simple as they made it seem in the movies, maybe then we neo-necromancers would sit atop this wretched earth.

As the warm liquor stung the involuntary muscles in my pharynx, I perched up, attempting to console my reclusive partner; Malach's cup had yet to leave the surface of the dining room table.

"*Dark brews for dark nights*, isn't that what you told me?"

"Indeed, but I don't care for it, at least not right now."

I turned back to the table with the scent of whiskey on my breath, "The tome?" He nodded and pressed his hands against his temples. "It is odd; why would your father have an empty book?"

"He wouldn't. My father had a fourth-grade education. Our home hadn't contained a single text. Certainly not something like...this." Malach inspected the bindings once more, however, the way his hand rubbed against the surface was almost sensual.

He was beginning to accept this book, or rather the book was beginning to accept him.

"If not from your father, then *who*?"

"Your guess is as good as mine. I bet that child has something to do with it though. Did you see his eyes?" I brought them to memory, the two abysmal holes carved in his sunken face. Malach shot from his chair and started pacing around the room. At the time, I could tell something had stricken him, yet I was unaware of how severe it was-if I knew what I did now, I would have stopped us here. Maybe things would have turned out different.

The whiskey settled my nerves as I consoled my suffering friend, "Talk to me."

His weary eyes fell upon the book, then back at me. "Does that...*sound* ring in your ears as well?"

"The television static? No, that doesn't faze me," I confessed while looking at the gray static cross the screen.

"No, it is a far-off droning. It sounds like…whispers."

"Whispers? Maybe the neighbors have their radio too loud?"

"It's faint but I can hear a voice. It...it sounds like...*my father's voice.*"

"When did it start?" I curiously asked as I tilted the bottle on the table.

"Since I opened the book. It's growing louder."

"Malach, do you feel something from the book?" He nodded, and finally placed the cup to his lips. He downed the first glass as one does after committing a horrid crime, and quickly poured himself another two cups.

"I've never felt such malevolence in my life. This desire for evil, it's overwhelming. This book…I don't think it was made by human hands. Now the whispers...they're trying to tell me something," Malach said while pointing to the book. His arm was wrapped around his chest as if he were on the verge of a heart attack.

At this time, I was curious to discover what malady had my partner gripped, for I'd not heard whispering or any bizarre noises. My fingers traced the outer lining of the book, running across the edges of teeth, hopping over a small gap that had enough space for one incisor. Even as I flipped through the thick pages my sanity remained wholly intact; but each page turn sent violent shudders through my partner.

Malach paused. His hands were vibrating like he'd been shocked, and there was a disastrous look upon his face, his eyes seemed to drift, rather than directly latching onto any visual anchors. "Bezel, can you honestly not hear them? They are *so loud.*" I disappointingly shook my head. Based on my immaturity in the realm of astral clairvoyance, I assumed that I was not yet adept enough to experience the sounds.

"They're so loud. Louder, LOUDER! MAKE THEM STOP! OH SATURN!" In a primal rage, Malach smashed the glass in his hands, and sent the objects on the dining room table, including the book, flying to the wooden floor. He then tore through the apartment, shirking away from invisible phantoms, howling madly. His spine contorted into a serpentine shape that no human (perhaps a world-class contortionist) could do without dislocating bones and discs. "I feel the talon of the black-winged one on my spine, caustic acid coursing through my nerves, the screeching of marrow rubbed against the base of my rotting skull." The sleeves from his robe were torn, and froth built up at his mouth; I'd wondered if he'd contracted a strain of rabies while we dissected the remains of that bat. "Was this how *The Betrayer* felt upon receiving his thirty pieces of silver?" he gurgled.

Suddenly, he stopped.

All that could be heard in the apartment was the exhalation of noxious air. Leaking from the corners of his thin lips was a trail of darkened blood that oozed on his shirt. I shouted at him to dislodge his bite, but it seemed that his joints had stiffened, experiencing a temporary bout of lockjaw.

Droplets splattered on his leather boots, exploding upon impact like a time-lapse of blooming roses. His skeleton then whipped back into frame, and pupils returned to their normal resting places-in the front of the skull. I realized whatever entity that possessed him was now exorcised.

He finally spoke. "What shall we say to Grand Wizard?"

"Grand Wizard? Malach, what about you!?" I medically inspected him while he stared at me with blank confusion. In the brown of his irises, I could tell he thought I was the irrational one. "What was that?!"

"What...do you mean?"

"The cursing, the scratching...you don't remember any of that?" By this time, he'd swirled enough blood throughout his mouth to know that it was his tongue he'd bit; the realization triggered in him slight tremors, but this onset was a pale comparison to what I'd previously witnessed. "What do you remember? Did you have a seizure?"

"Bezel, what are you talking about? We were in the middle of a conversation." Astonished, I spent the next several minutes describing to him, in great deal, his previous erratic actions; although shocked by the news, not for one second did he flinch as unbelievers do.

Silently, he cleaned up the apartment, placing the mats upon the table, drying the spilled whiskey, and removing the tatters hanging off his robe. Lastly, he raised the book from the base of the table, except this time he lifted it as if it weighed as much as a gray cinder block. I removed the paper towel used to wipe away the whiskey and set it against his cheeks which retained a shade of redness. My partner remained steady as I tended to his face. In this moment he was calm, he was Malach. I thought of asking about the whispers but did not wish to send him into a further spiral. His attention was caught by, what I foolishly assumed to be, the empty sheets.

"Can you see that?" he murmured.

"See what?"

"This…" his slender finger pointed directly towards the page.

Glancing past his split fingernail, my eyes registered markings on the page. Unidentifiable texts and hieroglyphic symbols that I'd only seen on the greater reaches of the dark web while researching the history of astral art. On the upper left corner, near the edge of the page, was a splotch of his blood. It then faded, as if absorbed by the tome.

"*One must give…to receive,*" Malach recited. It was one of the many rules that applied to arcane magic (and life, now that I think about it).

We both leaned into the book and examined, with bursting curiosity, the occultic symbols materializing. They sparsely resembled Arabic lettering but were written in a way that made it seem more cosmic than antediluvian.

"This is impossible to decipher. There has to be at least six different languages being used, and at least one lost to the human tongue." I confessed after trying for several minutes. My fingers rummaged through the volumes of sheets, but the other pages were still blank. "And why is this the only page visible? Is it a tradeoff? One drop for one spell?"

Malach mumbled under his breath while his fingers traced below the text. "*aluh, mgonka, tlues, gheszv, pralit, bhendt…Nox Eternis.*"

"Aluh what? More importantly, you can *read* that? What does it say?" The words trickled out of my trembling mouth.

Suddenly, he took a huge swig of the whiskey and bolstered his shoulders. His stature resembled that of a leader about to address his loyal troops before a suicide mission-and I was ready to follow him, even to the ends of the earth.

The tome was still upon the table, and to the side was the container of objects once bound to the lining of the front cover. "Bezel…we will no longer be bound to the arbitrary laws governing our primitive species. With this book, we will usher in the never-ending inferno, and finally show this feeble world our power. No more will we stand idle and let false prophets spread an incomplete gospel. We must purge the ignorant! By purging the corruption, we will surpass even the ancient atrocities inscribed in the famed Necronomicon.

"Upon these pages, I will strike a bargain." Removing the white feather, he dabbed at the blood leaking from the corner of his lips and placed his palm against the page. Within seconds his signature was upon the sheet, and the gray jewel flashed once, bathing the bleak apartment in mauve. "Transform me into a pure vessel for Saturn…, bless us with astral wisdom, and I promise to commit my soul to you, oh, shaded lords of the **Void!**"

"Malach!?" I finally shouted.

His ranting abruptly stopped and the flashes from the television screen cast a sinister glow on his face. Malach pressed his hands against the book cover, "The dead. Bezel…*we can raise the dead.*"

Zwei

Malach, humor me…why is this the first time I've heard of this book? Why was I not informed when it was initially retrieved? Do we not have open lines of communication; are you not supposed to inform your master when this was discovered? Dissemination." The voice of his master, the Grand Wizard, cracks in the PC speakers. His tone shifted from sympathetic to cynical. Bezel is unresponsive at first, expecting her partner to speak, but he remains perfectly still.

"I did share the book with my master. My true master, who taught me more than you ever did. I will say it again," Malach rises from his desk chair. He plants his eye inches away from the lens, staring intently into the device with a cyanotic eye. Or through it, into their screens. The swollen eye did not blink once for the thirty seconds he held the gaze. "This book is not meant for the feeble. I was chosen, me!" Malach states as he sits down at the PC. His face is sickly pale, blood covers his eardrums and malice laces his cheeks. "With me it will stay. The book has already *chosen* its vessel."

"You are merely an errand boy. Let us correct the error by passing it to me. As Grand Wizard, I am the most qualified to handle such magic."

His chapped lips form a tasteless smirk. "I believe you have been chosen, Roth. But not to be a paragon."

Roth's eyeliner smears when he rubs his face in frustration. "Quite the assumption, *my apprentice*; do not forget who noticed your potential. It was I who brought you to this point. When your father died, and you were wrought with grief over your grave sin, who was it that showed you the magic of Saturn? Who helped you cope and climb out of the grave of depression? Gave you purpose when all you wanted to do was waste away? I not only your master, I am your lord."

"I will not deny the validity of your claims, Roth. However, what is an apprentice but a successor to their master? There always comes a day…a day when the master is no longer essential to the apprentice. Grand Wizard, that day is *today*."

"Stop this useless banter, Malach. We have more important issues to discuss with the Grand Wizard. You said you wanted help, so let u-"

"I never requested any assistance!" Malach shouts; his upstairs neighbor responds by pounding the floor. A hacking cough expels a black glob of viscera from Malach's lips; the mucus crashes against his mouse. "You assumed I required aid, yet I have everything under control. Everything! I have already forgiven you for going behind my back to contact *him*. But, I digress, all will be revealed soon…one merely needs to wait."

"Your insolence will be forgiven, when you hand over the book," Roth counters.

"Do you think I want forgiveness for my actions? I have said nothing worth apologizing over; in fact, I believe I have spoken more clearly than I've ever wanted." Malach reclines in his desk chair, exhausted from preaching to the lost. He continues, "Grand Wizard, why is it that you never document your sinister feats? Not one recorded ritual in the past five years, out of a decade long career? Even my apprentice Bezel has documented three spellbinding activities. I'm quite curious, did you purposely avoid broadcasting them? Have you completed a hex this star cycle? Ever? One could say you're only a man with a title…a *false prophet.*"

"That is not your concern at this moment," Roth deflects.

"Oh, but it is! It's my only concern at this moment." The three screens glitch, simultaneously reacting to Malach's raised voice. The neighbor bangs again, this time longer and harder to drive the point home. "For four years, FOUR YEARS, I have followed your instructions, bowed my head without question; I served as your errand boy. Yet you kept my understanding of the **Void** to a minimum."

"That was to protect you, the forces that exist there are not to be reckoned with!"

"Indeed, by those who are ignorant." Dumbfounded, Roth fails to formulate a response. Malach continues to rant, "But now, with this book, I will transcend the Schism, become all-knowing like the paragons of Babylon. Oh Saturn, I thank thee for thy infinite blessings!

"Alas, Roth…there is more to learn. Bezel, please continue your tale." Salty orbs of sweat leaks from the Grand Wizard's pores; he tries to concentrate on Bezel's story, but a certain phrase scrapes against his skull.

False prophet.

I

Three days passed since the book came into our possession. I continued my normal routine at Crown & Roots while secretly procuring the ingredients from Malach's list. Since he was the only one able to understand the strange language, he provided translations. I managed to score a few of the vegetative items: camphor root, minced chaga mushrooms, *Conium maculatum* (hemlock) seeds, a vial of poisonous lobelia, two Mandrakes (I personally procured six from the internet); and the petals of a black dahlia. Each of these items alone had their uses in certain spells, but I questioned whether they would be effective in this scenario. They were common, so common that I started to doubt Malach; were his translations correct? Or had he sent me on a fool's errand while he toiled with the book?

There was also the matter of obtaining *a vessel*. Something that Malach and I had yet to discuss...

A few customers came by during those three days, most of them were of the gossiping elderly, which is customary. There is little activity in a town of less than 3,000 so the elders entertain themselves by sharing the latest hearsay. The current story circulating through everybody's tongues was that of Miranda's mysterious murder. On Monday, Mrs. Janice, who was a regular attendee of bingo, claimed that she overheard from one of her church members that Miranda was "bumpin biscuits" with the current coach of the softball team. Apparently, jealousy was the M.O. behind the killing. Mrs. Janice ended up purchasing a handful of ginkgo for her dementia, so I chose not to trust her information.

The man who had found her, Horace, also came by the store to purchase lavender for his room. He claimed the sight of her body shook him so much that he's had trouble sleeping ("and the bottle ain't strong enough to stop this."). Naturally, I probed the man for intimate details. Information was traded for a discount on lavender, which is quite expensive during the cold season-longer nights, less light. Withholding nothing from me, Horace expressed in his Midwestern drawl the facts of the murder. At first, I was engrossed in his story, believing that I was the sole holder of secret information; halfway through, I realized that he was reiterating the same story he told the news anchor. It was dramatized to the point that I could no longer tell the fiction from the fact-it also should be stated that poor Horace suffers from severe PTSD.

I was about to write him off and continue tending to the potted plants until the senile veteran uttered a cryptic statement: "*She ain't even have a face*. All I seen was the stuff that sits in the skull, and that ain't supposed to be seen by no man. Destroyed, that's what it was. I done seen many a dead man but never that. A killing like that? True evil, ain't no doubt about it. Careful, the devil doesn't walk among us, *only within us*." Horace departed with his purchase, but his closing statement lingered throughout the entire seven-hour shift.

I'd not known Miranda personally, but for someone to have their face "destroyed" was a horrible way to die. And yet, I was instinctively drawn to the misfortune surrounding her murder. Further inquiry would require access to the internet; charged with apprehension and morbid curiosity, I scurried straight to library after clocking out in the afternoon.

The walls of the library were an ugly shade of cream and lacked any decorative work, except for one painting. It was of a distant sea caught in a tumultuous and gray storm. Impressionistic in style, the artwork was well-crafted but sorely out of place. It only escalated my frustration as my searches remained fruitless. I'm ashamed to even categorize this low-budget, community college-sized classroom as a library, but it is the only location in Lindsborg where individuals have access to public computers. When it comes to my studies regarding the dark magic, I prefer to do them on the public domain rather than my personal laptop-to avoid any digital paper trails. There were few books lining the shelves of the library; so few that one could peer right through the manuscripts and spy on another. Only a few individuals populated the library at this hour, which was the case for each hour it was open. Seated across the room, near the droning water fountain, was a duo of high school students tinkering on a project, an alarmingly quiet construction worker struggled to remain awake while reading a book on personal finance, and the librarian whose turkey sweater had enough Thanksgiving paraphernalia to decorate the entire town was restacking checked in books.

My initial objective was to uncover details regarding Miranda, in both her life and death. For possibly an hour, maybe two, I rummaged through posts, pages, wall scrawling, tagged photos, timelines, and feeds to find out everything I could, and I did-unsettling how the deceased continue to exist digitally. I learned Miranda was born with a hormonal disease, which accounted for her hulking frame and social awkwardness. She'd also been a recurrent patient at the pediatric hospital in Topeka; her disease became a regional case study which generated the attention of many endocrinologists.

At the time of her death, she'd been 'close' with the softball coach of the Lindsborg Lions, who appeared in several pictures with the girl. There were plenty of puppy love poses: sharing ice cream cones on a bench, two bats and a softball, movie ticket stubs. I envied her; even she found someone to love her despite her flaws. Sorrow overtook me as I continued my search; the more I learned, the more I wished we could've met…even been friends. My research regarding Miranda's life had been fulfilling; however, my search regarding clues about her death was the opposite. Every news outlet covered the story the same way, with a portrait and a tip line. The police had yet to release a statement or a list of suspects, holding off an official investigation; hopefully waiting for potential evidence...or a second murder.

Realizing that I'd learned all I could about the subject, I decided to switch my inquiry. Although the grimoire was nameless, the physical appearance was so bizarre I figured at least one other individual had to share something on the internet. I resorted to Google; spent nearly thirty minutes seeking any information, however, I reached a dead end with every clicked link.

During my browsing, I noticed the high schoolers staring at me. Nearly twenty-four, I'd consider myself somewhat attractive, and a few brave individuals have dared to attempt a relationship with me. The last boyfriend I had was a local grown farmer who said very little, but there was a light in his eyes whenever he listened to me rant about my sorrows. I share this personal information because I recognized the same glimmer in the gaze of the two boys. And suddenly, I was set ablaze, heated from the inside out. My core temperature probably rose to a hundred degrees in ten seconds. The room became a spiral, and I felt my digested food trying to exit-one way or the other. I pulled my maroon sweater over my head to catch my breath but when I popped it off the boys had already vanished. Along with whatever malady had swept over me in that short period.

I examined myself as if I had survived a bomb barrage, touching every part of my body to determine if the pieces were present. However, my exam was cut short when the turkey-faced librarian quietly informed me that the library would be closing in the next fifteen minutes. With that in mind, I attempted one last sweep of the internet, which meant it was time to go on the dark web.

The digital world is full of laws, most of which we believe to understand, but new technology is greater than our current comprehension, so loopholes exist. There are places that one is not supposed to venture unless they desire *the truth*. Not the regurgitated opinions regarded by the majority, but rather valid explanations for the questions that plague humanity. To seek this truth is to dip into the darkness, for anything worth discovering is hidden there.

Utilizing a specific portal on an onion browser, my screen was directed to the Glass Dungeon, a site like Reddit on the dark web except it pertains to the arcane and occult. Most modern magicians are aware of the Glass Dungeon, the vault of arcane and ancient information compiled over centuries. Here, one can find evidence of mass disappearances happening around the world, alien technology being reverse engineered, doomsday cults recruiting new members, government conspiracies about fluoride, and a host of other offbeat knowledge. Many "normal" citizens believe this to be impractical information, but it is wise to be aware of all possibilities. However, in all its wisdom on the occult, it seemed even the Glass Dungeon had little to report on the tome.

My palms ran hot as I furiously typed; truly, had no person heard of this book? Maybe, just maybe, my partner lied…No, he wouldn't do that. After all, I trusted Malach like no other (although my mom is a close second). He granted wishes and ushered me to the gates of the dark world; without him, I can say, wholeheartedly, I'd be lost.

A hand tapped the computer twice; each tap sent another line of static across the screen. Turning swiftly in the chair I came face to face with the owner of the hand: one of the teenage boys, the other was sitting next to me, playing some flight simulator. There was something different about them, the boys looked very similar, possible twins. The "drummer" standing next to my computer grinned stretching ear to ear while the other rose from his seat and gave the bird to the screen. He then rotated the chair until he faced my computer and tapped the monitor with his hand.

The display de-rezzed for an instant and returned with a high-res picture of the grimoire; it was impossible to miss those teeth. Finally, an anchor to bind me on this endless digital sea. The instant I clicked on the link, the two boys sprinted out the exit, throwing down books as they departed and catching the anger of the librarian. But her verbal assault was immediately halted by a thunderous boom that originated from outside, in the direction the two boys ran. I wanted to investigate further, but with roughly two minutes left before the librarian ordered me to leave ("When it's closing time, it's closing time," as mother says), I decided to focus on short sentences and italicized words.

"I've heard this contains the spell called Raloevla; it's what the druids used to revive Lancelot and imbue him with invulnerability."

"Opened a portal to Arthishia, the world of destruction, where I spent seven hundred years as a divine emissary. But upon my return, I realized by body had not aged a day. Now all I desire is rest, but the book won't let me."

"Has anybody him them?? The one with the black eyes? That boy...he keeps following me. I see him everywhere, and all he does is stare. But...I don't think he's alone either."

"We enthralled the entire village with one spell. We drowned them in the ocean as an offering to the gods of wisdom."

"This book has the power to summon the most torturous of demons. But I haven't been able to stop the whispers. Please, someone make them stop!"

"Nox Eternis... Nox Eternis..."

"It was used to cast the illusion over Ingilaef, enshrouding the mystical realm with a reflective material that prevents those unworthy from visiting. But it also has imprisoned those within."

"This tome makes murder mundane. There are acts of suffering that the human spirit cannot fathom, and this book holds the answers to that."

"It is forbidden magic. Your soul will be lost to the **Void** *when you accept the contract. The sign is only a facade, the real contract is the teeth. Once it has that, you are bound. Permanently."*

Anxiety pulsed through my elastic arteries, why were there no definite answers? This forced me to base my opinion on the testimony of others, and I could not find a common ground within any story. Utilizing the last seconds of public internet access, I constructed a message on the Glass Dungeon asking for any information. Afterwards I felt foolish, how many others probably performed the same action, and received no response.

The intercom system from City Hall blasted outside, signaling the approach of five P.M. After picking up the books dropped by the brats, the turkey librarian announced the official closing of the library and glared at me with one of those passive-aggressive stares only women from the Midwest can master (a skill my mother has yet to pass to me). Dissatisfied with my detective skills, I left the library sulking with an ardent agitation in my heart. Not only had I failed myself, but I'd failed Malach, who was in desperate need of answers. Ever since the arrival of the book his demeanor changed from stoic to erratic with the zeal of a deranged religious leader. I feared I was losing him to something...something so powerful it couldn't have originated from human hands.

II

The sun drowsily set over the harvested fields, casting an autumn aura across the horizon over the grainy sea; amorphous insects frolicking like puff balls blown by wishful lips. Sights like these reminded me of childhood days spent with my brother, Victor. He was older by three years and shaped his character in the likeness of James Dean: roguish facial features and a strong jaw line and yet sensitive eyes and lips that produced more cries than curses. It was in these moments that my admiration for my brother was at an all-time high, he'd stare his fears directly in the face with a cocky smile and challenge them without any regard. I genuinely loved my brother; but, affection was an affliction to him.

Victor was cursed with a terrible case of manic depression at age eleven due to a traumatic incident car accident involving a decapitated head-the driver of a pick-up truck had veered into the lane and caused a head-on collision. Victor happened to be riding front seat with my father in the car. Both of them survived relatively unscathed (my father did manage to break a toe and a collarbone). However, the sight of the headless body stumbling out of the wreckage of the white pick up scarred my brother in ways that we could never understand. I think he realized a truth about life: that it can be magical and fulfilling and in one instant it can be ended, painfully. After that, he spent most afternoons locked in the tool shed, where he would spend countless hours reading biographies of famous writers until dinner-he called the shed a safe house for sinners. But the days he dared to venture out of his haven were unforgettable. What courage he expressed, choosing to live with his demons.

However, his departure came swift, and with such a sorrow that I have yet to process it. One night Victor broke into the gun case my father kept for the occasional coyote, after my family fell into a food coma. He crept out of the bedroom, the pistol loaded and tucked into his flannel onesie. Something stirred me awake, probably the sound of the back door shutting (my room was directly above). From my bed I peered out the window and went on high alert when I saw a light outside. The door of the shed was partially opened; Victor occasionally visited the shed at odd hours of the night when his insomnia was flaring, but never was the door left open.

Before I drew back the curtain and tried to fall asleep again, a bomb of sonic energy detonated. And then an agonizing cry bled out of the shed onto the granite cornerstone, between the damp floorboards, through the power sockets and ventilation grates, and along the creases of the ceiling before nailing into my ear. Nausea had its way with my stomach as the muscles in my throat constricted to the point of suffocation. Without having to investigate the room adjacent to mine, I knew-by some otherworldly sense that siblings possess-Victor was in trouble.

A second gunshot muted the harrowing cry.

Muffled voices rumbled below my bedroom; the sound had awakened my parents. The shed illuminated our backyard like a cursed lantern. I held my breath for moments, waiting for a signal. For Victor to waltz back out of the shed with that silver dollar smile. The backdoor open again, and my father appeared in the field below my window. The ephemeral light beckoned him to the shed. He hobbled towards the structure, baseball bat in hand; pushed the door open slowly. The bat fell out of his hands as he rushed in with a guttural "NO!".

I don't know why I went to the shed…I was wholly aware of what I'd find beyond that wooden door, in the brilliance of the cursed lantern. Perhaps I needed visual proof, as most humans require if they are to truly believe. My feet darted out of the bed, down the flight of stairs without a stumble, and out onto the damp grass. Before I reached the shed a gargantuan hand yanked me to the ground. Wrestling followed this body slam, but I squirmed out of his flaccid grip and dashed to the shed-some nights, I wish my father had been a stronger man and stopped me. This was the first time, but not the last, I witnessed my father break down and cry.

Across the yellow wallpaper inside the toolshed was a vast blossom of warm blood; droplets leaked from the tips of my father's metals tools. The emergency (cursed) lantern was shelved next to paint cans-usually this was kept in the linen closet down the hall from our bedrooms. Two, empty 9mm shell casing were tucked underneath the gas generator, the pistol resting peacefully upon a palm. A palm belonging to a body slumped underneath the crimson graffiti. And the body belonged to Victor.

The scaly hands of my father covered my eyes before I was able to see anything else, but what I witnessed was already burned into my brain. His chin, lower jaw, lips, four front teeth and nose were missing, completely blown away by a point-blank pistol. The misfire. Victor's death devastated my family, not only emotionally but financially. An immense debt was slapped on us after the expensive funeral. As I wandered from the library to my car, I felt a stinging in my gut. The sights of the Thanksgiving decorations tore my spirit with each step, had twelve years truly passed since that tragic day?

A boyish giggle dispelled the memories, and I turned to find both high school students once again. As I examined them (a retail skill), I was mesmerized by their symmetry. *Twins*? There was only one pair of high school twins in Lindsborg: Dan and Dave Hamilton. And these two boys did not resemble them in the slightest (Dan and Dave wore dusty overalls with no underwear). Their attire also raised multiple questions, both students donned identical outfits (cliché twin behavior). I registered the misty white blouses, and strange placement of the jewels on the tailored pants; they bared a striking resemblance to the garments worn by the enigmatic boy waiting for us with the book. Maybe Malach and I were being recruited by some esoteric organization-I'd heard of certain necromantic guilds employing "extreme" forms of hazing-and these strangers could've been lackeys of the hidden order.

But then the twins turned to me, and I saw their eyes. *Black as the* **Void**.

"Do you have two smokes?"

"Are you afraid of dying?"

The two spoke almost simultaneously, yet it sounded as if they shared one voice. "How do you know I smoke? And no, I'm not afraid," I proudly stated.

"The stains on your teeth."

"And you smell like ashes."

Embarrassed, I removed the crumpled pack from my back pocket and handed each of them one. Oddly enough, they both took a cigarette with the opposing hand. "Are you two old enough to be smoking? I don't want to get in trouble."

"Indeed *I* am, and there will be no trouble"

"If you read the book."

"Has she read it though?"

"Doubtful, she would know *who I am*."

"Right! She should read the book."

"The book was made to be read."

"You know what book we speak of."

"The book knows you. It will help you."

"But one must give…"

"…in order to receive."

"Make an offering."

"And the book will choose you."

I paused for it was my intention to consider this a ruse being pulled by bored high schoolers. Youth are notorious for mischief and will often carry a prank to the point of endangering the victim. That'd been the case with Miranda prior to the state championship game. In perfect sync, the two boys turned their heads to peer into each other's eyes before honing their sights to me. "Why should I read the book?" I asked. I became nervous, not because I believed my life to be in danger, but because lurking questions were about to be answered.

"It waits for your eyes."

"Because you don't know about it."

"I can change that."

"If you really want to know."

"I'll give you two questions…"

"…for the two smokes. Use them wisely."

I was about to spill my first question, to inquire about its origin but the eerie twins raised their hands simultaneously, operating as chiral carbon copies of each other.

"I will not answer it now."

"Where's the fun in instant gratification?"

"I need to see how bad you want to know."

"You must wait until we meet *again.*"

The two boys wildly danced along the sidewalk like warlocks worshipping a foxfire under a blood moon; accessories jingling like wind chimes made of noble metals disturbed by the gust. Just like the delivery boy, the duo bowed and then ran in opposing directions to confuse me. One turned down Main street while the other ran toward the hospital. Both of them disappeared within minutes, but I had no desire to give chase; I had all the information I needed (or rather all the information they were willing to let me have at this time).

My shoulders relaxed as my apprehension departed with them. The mysterious duo may have acted like any pubescent teenagers looking for a rise, but the entire interaction felt as if they were dumbing themselves down for my comfort, as if I were too immature in my understanding to behold them in their authentic visage. I realized a terrifying plot had been hatched, and, we were merely pawns on their board.

III

"Malach, this ritual. Are you sure you want to go through with it?" I announced when entering his apartment. The place still bared scars from his previous ransacking; perhaps more chaos had ensued over the past three days. I placed my basket of the ingredients on his kitchen table, and strolled through the complex, unable to locate him. Taking care not to tread upon any fragments, my feet carefully glided across the floor until I came to his bedroom.

Normally, the acidic scent of formaldehyde, from the morgue, lingered in the bedroom, but today it had a sweet scent like honey. Peering through the opened doorway, my eyes identified familiar objects: the owl bust he'd purchased from a traveling taxidermist after our first seance, Aquarius crystals used for soothsaying, a notebook containing our five-year plan for our page on the Glass Dungeon; and the digital camera we purchased for the purpose of documenting our mystical feats (it was also Malach's unofficial birthday gift).

With the agility of a thief, I slipped through the crack in the doorway and entered the bedroom; curiosity called me to the camera. Malach's goal was to spread the name of Saturn throughout the earth, and this he accomplished by running a domain on the Glass Dungeon. Even in the desolate town of Lindsborg, we were able to generate a following of sixty-four devoted followers who gather online to express their genuine love for necromancy. My fingers ran across the power switch of the camera. Greeted with the faint glow of the LED screen I decided to take a glance at the saved pictures.

Scrolling through the camera brought me a bittersweet grief; each image transported me to a specific memory shared with Malach. He'd inspired me to live unapologetically, the same way my brother instilled into me his desire for life despite the anguish. As the screen flashed I thought of Victor again. How good of friends he and Malach would have been if they'd met. Both were so true to their will, ready to tackle even the most unknowns of the unknown equipped with unwavering faith in the presence of sorrow. Or...maybe they would have been at each other's throat, for men of extreme virtue are, by nature, solitary creatures.

My eyes registered a new sight on the rectangular screen: the date read today. With apprehension wrapped upon my neck like a thick noose, I clicked the button marked "PLAY". The video was out of focus, however it soon autocorrected, establishing the location. I immediately recognized the rings of Saturn poster; Malach had it hung in his living room. A few quiet seconds passed and then a ghastly figure appeared on the left side of the screen. Coming closer towards the center, the silhouette finally materialized. The hood of the robe enshrouded the figure's face, but underneath the darkness I could see a steeled resolve, the same resolve expressed by my dear partner, Malach.

Our camera's speaker had been damaged during a botched recording of a hexing, rendering the sound useless; this made it difficult for me to listen to the words he chanted. It seemed to be English, saying something like: lords of the **Void**. Suddenly, his jaw twitched, and he spoke in languages long forgotten to the modern tongue.

On the dining room table, next to a misplaced hardware tool, was the book that seemed to have restored a great deal of color to its cover. The lubricating solution oozing from its textured spine was viscous, and the teeth were...whiter. He removed the text from the table we'd regularly ate at and placed it upon his lap. The book opened to a page-I'd wager that it was the same page that drank his blood. His attention was upon the lettering for an uncomfortably long time, glaring as if he were an ancient sage deciphering an immortal message.

Malach removed his hood. How sickly he looked, his soul suffocating in a fermenting miasma. Orifices covered in crust, and eyes swollen and bloodshot like a cinema zombie. Sluggishly, Malach proceeded to undress. Gripping the camera, I realized this was the first time I'd seen his body, but what it revealed was more than prolonged desires. Fresh red whelps ran parallel across his chest and strange jagged patterns had been deeply etched into his pectoral muscles. The sight was truly horrifying in detail, but upon focusing I realized a much greater danger. There was thought put into this carving of flesh; Malach had inscribed "runes" into his skin and intended to use his body as a conduit.

As you know, runes are required in many rituals for it compresses the energy required for a spell; however, they are typically inscribed in specialized ore or sacred wood. During the primitive years of necromancy, bodies were occasionally used for the vilest of spells, yet they were often corpses; necromancers themselves never channeled the energy directly. I recognized the pre-Germanic lettering, but it was far more complex than any symbols I'd seen.

Malach uttered another impossible to interpret phrase while his hand lay pressed against the page. When his lips finally stopped moving, his gaze turned toward the camera.

Watching from the comfort of the desk, I peered out of Malach's bedroom into the living room as an arachnid shutter crawled up my spine; had all of this transpired within these four walls? When my attention returned to the camera, I locked onto Malach's eyes. He stared at the camera as if cognizant I'd be watching this recording. His left hand reached across the table and removed the tool, which appeared to be a pair of rusted pliers. Malach briefly examined them, noting the bright blue rubber handle before bringing the metallic clamps to his mouth. The pliers latched to his left central incisor.

With a demonic force, Malach pulled the tooth. And suddenly the camera shrieked; somehow the unwanted sound returned. His wails of agony sent me into a minor panic. What anguish there was in my partner's voice; a blood-curdling scream erupting from the space between the bone and the being. And the extraction of the tooth. The awful tearing of roots, snapping like stumps exhumed from dry soil. The sound disappeared, leaving me with a gruesome visual; he'd dropped to his knees by this point, but the tooth was hanging out of his drooling mouth by a single tendon. He then wrapped both bloody hands around the incisor, exhaled and-

Abruptly, the screen went black, and the text "DEAD" appeared over the battery graphic. Was there a point to search for the battery charger, or had I witnessed enough brutality to appease my wonder? I dropped the camera on the desk and slowly exited the room, unable to douse the screams previously witnessed. Harrowing, like Victor's wails.

Back in the living room I searched the scene of the snuff film, perceiving the stained pliers with a new sense of dread. A puddle of dried blood formed where he'd been kneeling, the iron odor circulated in the ventilation. A makeshift trail of hemoglobin led my sights to the tome, which sat with its cover closed. The gap once between the incisors was now filled…with a reddened tooth. Horrified, I turned back to the vacant apartment until my eyes laid upon the source of this suffering. Sitting on the couch, obscured by darkness, was Malach. He sat as if he'd been present all along, waiting for me.

The first thing that I noticed about my friend was that he seemed to be in particularly high spirits, which was rare. Was this the same person who had committed that atrocious self-mutilation, or the man who'd taught me of Saturn's secrets? He'd never been a depressive or overly melancholic, but he hardly portrayed vibrant emotions. Jeremy Thomas had raised his son to be a resolute observer, to contain his emotions inside a titanium lock box and then lose the key to it. But the man standing in front of me joyfully grinned, which made me quite unsteady.

Malach was the first to break the silence. "Did you procure the ingredients?" I pointed to the basket brought from my store. "Good, the hour of our ascension approaches."

"Malach, are you…" I gazed at the gap between his smile and nearly gagged. If I accused him, then who would I have left? Was I willing to break that bond? "I…I trust you. I don't necessarily know what's going on, but I trust you will do what's right. I won't ask any more questions."

What was the point? The determination I saw in his eyes rivaled the spirit of the immortal heroes from the great Homeric epics; no amount of words I spewed could alter his mind. However, the forewarning from the twins echoed in my heart, and I found myself bound to inquire about our ritual. "What else…do you need for the spell?" I asked.

"I have created the necessary rune." He meant his body.

"What of our location? What sort of place could possibly manifest the energy we require? This is…this is an advanced spell."

"We will use a place steeped in death, a home to hollow eyes and hearts drenched with embalming fluid. *We will use the morgue.* I have already prepared the site and drafted the transmutation circles."

Malach rose from the couch and his limp arms barely managed to wrap around me. I don't know why, but suddenly I found my heart beating like the hooves of a mustang galloping full speed. "My dear Bezel, have you considered what we will do as masters of this new world?" His arms were light like porous bones, and the pallor in his skin made him more akin to the corpses he cleaned for the county.

"I haven't. I don't…well, I don't mind what we do…if we're together." Would emotions be able to pierce the veil that shrouded Malach's eyes?

"There will be no force known to man that will separate us. Once we complete our ritual, we will have dominion over everything, including death." His hands stroked the cover of the tome as if it were a newborn babe whom he'd brought into the world. How different things were after the delivery of this book. "Before we continue, you must immortalize your conviction."

Malach removed the container from the cover of the tome and placed it on the table, "You must sign, and then you must make an offering." He meant a tooth.

Knowing what I did about the book, which was very little, I still drew the weighted needle and feather from the container. "If I…if we do this, can we take a break? Go on a trip? I've always wanted to leave Kansas, and I've almost saved up enough money. Let's go…just to see the world, what lies beyond the state line. We can buy a train ticket to anywhere, or just rent a car and drive east. I've heard of a city made of oaks. Imagine, trees as tall as buildings..."

A wave of dissatisfaction washed across Malach's face; ambition was to blame for his intolerance. He remained motionless for the next few seconds, my wishful muttering reached a painful end, and I accepted the silence as a valid response. My worries mutated into tangible anxiety; this book, this otherworldly force had enough power to subjugate even the Midwestern magician of the macabre. What chance did I stand? Once we would've spent this day facilitating the occasional summoning, or experimenting with illusory magic, or enlightening other lost souls drifting through the sea of absurdity. But…this book changed everything. Now, we were on a downward spiral to the abyss, and I feared nothing could save us now.

The prick of a needle is a different type of pain, a precise attack that causes the nerves to violently react, a scraping that one feels between their toes. A bead of blood leaked out of the invisible hole between my epidermal cells. Taking hold of the vulture feather, I was amazed not by its lustrous color, but rather its weight. It felt as if I were holding a mechanical pen, significantly heavier than any quill I'd ever used. My mother brags about my signature whenever we shop together, saying to every clerk that I have the "Best Handcock on the Northern Hemisphere" (a horrid title). That is because I take pride in my name and relish any opportunity I must write it.

I thought back to the portal on the Glass Dungeon, and the random blurbs of info. I didn't want to sign it, not after learning what I did. But…the look on Malach's face, the unquestionable joy that beamed from his gapped smile made me throw away all logic. The tip of the quill pierced the page of the book, and slowly curled and undulated its way from one letter to the next until…

Malach raised his eyebrow. "…Ah, I understand. That is your real name. You chose to offer your real name and not your astral identity?"

"You told me to sign! Wait…no! Malach, what does this mean…no tell me. What happens if I give them my real name? Malach! What does it mean?"

"Truthfully…I do not know. But if you wish to tap into the wellspring of cosmic power, then you must offer more." The weight of the pliers dropped my arm; the handle still had a handprint from Malach's blood. "With this, we will become ushers of a new age."

He waited for me to commit the act, to self-mutilate and extract my own tooth without anesthesia or even liquor. But his waiting turned to impatience and suddenly my partner attempted to snatch the pliers. His hands came with fury, but none of them were fists or even had a hint of violence behind them; they were simply seeking the pliers. The violence would happen after he obtained them. Maybe he intended to pull my teeth himself, but I did not grant him the chance. In self-defense, I swatted with the pliers. The rusted metal connected to the side of his temple and the five-foot eleven-inches man dropped to the ground. Unconscious.

The tension dissolved and I dropped the tool. I then looked at the book and saw it. *Natalie*. My name…my real name, signed in my real blood. In a fit fueled by frustration, I snapped the feather and slammed the book shut. If Malach had been more affluent and resided in an apartment equipped with a fireplace, I would've tossed the infernal tome into the furnace.

After cooling down, I thought about moving Malach to a more comfortable position, but fear of his unconscious body coming to life and assaulting me again proved too great. He'd be fine on the floor. Quietly, I exited his apartment and drove home, my path guided by the streetlights and stars; but was this enough light to guide us out of this hell? I thought about my partner, and how I could possibly apologize for the hit, or what other actions could I do to help him through this…but my mind continued to deter on the drive home. Every thought eventually mutated into one: Now I belonged to the book too.

Drei

Septum Bezel, you have done well to share this much with me," Grand Wizard Roth states with a frightening degree of anger, concealed by gritted teeth. "Malach, why did you conduct a high-level ritual without first informing me? Was that not our agreement, that I was to know of all astral activities? And yet, you intentionally chose to disobey."

"I did, because I'd rather not waste my words on the worthless. Roth, *you are no Grand Wizard.* You have the funds to dress the part, and the education to speak eloquently, but you are no servant of Saturn. Thankfully, I have been ordained to lead the purge against false prophets. He checks the clock on his screen, "Seems we are out of time." Malach rises from the chair in his apartment and walks away from the field of vision of the webcam. This renders the image insignificant emphasizing the audio: the opening of a kitchen drawer, zippers locking on a bookbag, the clipping of a black jacket (Malach's only jacket), and, jingling of his apartment keys adorned with the severed and dressed foot of a black hare.

"Where are you going? Did you forget the town is looking for you?" Bezel scans the room for her overcoat. "If you're leaving… then I'm going too."

"Septum Bezel, halt! You have not yet finished explaining what has transpired. If you desire my aid, then I require knowledge; I need to know exactly what happened. You leave now, and I will be forced to withdraw my aid."

Gradually, Bezel returns to focus and sighs. "My apologies, I will conclude my story, so we can act with haste."

|

The intended day of the ritual, if it were still to be done, arrived with haste. I'd not seen Malach over the last two days, for Thanksgiving kept me preoccupied and I figured it was best for us to have space after the incident. I won't mention much regarding this holiday; traditionally, it is a somber moment. Not only did my family fall victim to gluttony by eating an unnecessarily costly dinner, but the anniversary of Victor's death passed. He'd taken his life on this day…on Black Friday.

This lingering grief kept me bedridden for much of the morning, and, unfortunately, I was late for my shift at Crown & Roots. It is one thing to be an employee running late, and another to be a keyholder running late. On the rare occasions when I arrived five minutes (maybe seven) late, there were a few impatient customers lined up at the entrance, tapping their feet noisily. However, today there were no patrons, only two men dressed in uniforms. Their badges flashed as I approached the entrance. What were the police doing at my store?

I hastened my step when one of the officers caught sight of me. He tapped his partner on the shoulder and nodded in my direction. "Morning gentlemen, can I interest you in any honey for your donuts?"

"Not today, ma'am. Although that does sound rather tempting."

"Did something happen to the store, Sheriff…Mangat?" He tipped his hat forward and glanced at the store's façade. Mangat had hazel eyes that sunk into his hairless head. He dressed in a thermal covered by a windbreaker issued to the entire police department (which was only about thirty members), and a pair of cargo khakis. And his work boots were shined with the utmost care. Most of the police force in Lindsborg can be considered "green behind the ears," for the town rarely dealt with serious crime; Mangat was the sole exception. He'd previously worked with the missing persons department at the Kansas State Bureau of Investigation for nearly two decades and moved to Lindsborg after completing a five-year cold case, involving a human trafficking ring.

"Nope, store's fine. We got a few questions for you, if you don't mind. Ms…?"

"Natalie. You can call me Natalie. And it's no problem at all." At this time, I was unaware if I stuttered or not.

The second deputy stepped forward with a notebook that had been purchased at a convenience store; definitely a green-eared, the crumbs on his uniform gave him away. "Deputy Harold Larson." He introduced himself with an unwanted pat on my shoulder. Larson's black hair was clogged with grease that poured down his moon face, giving the appearance of a perpetual sweat. The fact that his windbreaker was too sizes too small didn't help; he looked like a bobblehead. "Now, Miss Natalie, are you associated with a Mr. Nicolas Thomas?"

"Mr. Thomas?"

Dumbfounded Larson looked at me as if I'd made some poor joke. "Nicolas? Caretaker at the morgue. The townspeople claim you two are a couple. Inseparable lunatics who are perfect for each other-according to Mrs. Janice."

"Right. *Nicolas*…slipped my mind. Did something happen to him?" I wondered if Malach's fate had come sooner than expected? He'd been alone on Thanksgiving, and in a state so vulnerable that I would not be surprised if he'd inflicted some mortal wound upon himself. I feared that I was to blame, and torrent of depression coursed through my bloodstream.

Deputy Larson spat his glob of dip into a small patch of grass, "He's missing."

Mangat glared at him, revealing evidence was a rookie mistake. This town trusted each other too much. "…What my partner meant to say was Nicolas has been absent from work for the past two days. Each phone call has been met with a dial tone."

"He was supposed have the Marshalls body prepared for the wake, which is this afternoon," Deputy Larson commented. "Guess it doesn't matter if we have a body, the casket's gonna be closed regardless. No way they'd show that mug to anybody."

Visibly annoyed at his partner, Sheriff Mangat shifted his broad shoulders, assuming a more assertive pose. "Have you been in contact with Mr. Thomas recently? Anything at all? Even a message?"

"Not since earlier this week. I saw him Monday, maybe Tuesday, but haven't heard from him since. Holidays kept me busy."

The pen in Deputy Larson's hand scribbled furiously on the pad. "How did he seem last time you talked to him?" Mangat inquired.

"Mostly tired. Work had been taking a toll on him recently. He was in the process of sketching out upgrades for the morgue but frustrated because the state was withholding funding."

"I see, so work had him pretty stressed out?"

"I'd say so. He's the only one down there, you know. It's not easy to work what he does; to care for the dead."

"Care for the dead…" Larson repeated.

Mangat crouched under the roof of Crown & Roots and advanced towards me, utilizing his stature as a means of intimidation-I could smell his cheap shaving gel. "Did Mr. Thomas ever do anything...to the bodies? He ever tell you any stories? Maybe poor jokes?"

"No, he cared for all of the remains with care. He is a thorough and dedicated disciple. Why would you make that accusation?" I scoffed.

Both officers awkwardly shuffled around in their respective spaces, and an unsettling tingle coated my appendages. I was doing too much.

Sheriff Mangat rubbed his face twice and tapped his walkie-talkie before addressing me. *"The body of Miranda Marshalls is missing."*

I stepped back, not out astonishment, but out of acknowledgment. Malach was determined to complete the ritual, and he'd overcome every obstacle thus far with tact and logic. "How do you know?"

"We…we found-her toe tag at the scene," Mangat said,

"Still attached to her toe," Deputy Larson added.

"But not the rest of her," Mangat completed.

"Do you think Ma… Mr. Thomas had anything to do with this?"

"We aren't sure yet ma'am, just trying to gather evidence. The coroner was helping us work the Marshalls case; he was scheduled to visit the morgue and conduct an autopsy Thursday."

"Some carve turkeys on Thanksgiving; others carve *bodies*," Deputy Larson muttered under his breath.

Sheriff Mangat continued, "But he failed to return home last night. His wife just came by the station today to report the incident." I nearly lost my breakfast at the mention of "wife."

Townsfolk gathered on the opposing side of the street; eavesdropping was a community activity in Lindsborg. Betty Janice, decked out in her faux leather parka and Kohl's capris, was among the crowd of petty nannies and retirees with nothing better to do with their time than gawk and peck at situations that didn't involve them. Ironically she ran the town's intercom system from City Hall. Both officers waved for them to move along, but the gossipers held their ground.

"When we arrived at the morgue, it looked as if an…altercation occurred. Maybe a break in, or scuffle, we're not sure."

Deputy Larson interjected. "Another question: Seen anything like this?" Mangat rubbed his temples as Larson flipped through the notebook. He then tilted the page towards me. "We found these at the crime scene." To conceal my involvement in this matter, I remained completely unphased by the crude sketching; but, sure enough, the image sketched on the page was a transmutation circle.

"Yes, that's a transmutation circle. It's used in alchemy…" the more I spoke the more I started to sound guilty. Larson furrowed his brow and let his pen fly over the notebook at the word "alchemy". Clearly ignorant of the importance of this drawing to not only the sages of arcane arts but those also invested in the esoteric. "I know because I watch an anime, a Japanese cartoon, that uses them," I added the Japanese to clear the confusion.

"There's speculation that devil worship is at play. Heard talks of Satanists coming into the Midwest, pourin in like immigrants. They routing the devils to our good land." Deputy Larson's assumptions leaked into the conversation.

Mangat steadied his hand, he was upset with his partner. He then brought the conversation back to its original focus while Green-ear scribbled more in his notebook. "Incident could be related to the Marshalls case; maybe the suspect is trying to cover their tracks. Possibility that Mr. Thomas and the coroner were caught in the confrontation. Not sure."

"We won't hold you up much longer, but if you think of something give us a call. We'd appreciate it." Deputy Larson wiped the dip spit from his chin and placed his flimsy business card in my hand. A gust of wind blew through the dead foliage, uncanny crackles echoed in the vacant street.

"No further questions. Thank you again, ma'am. I'll be back to try some of that homegrown honey," Sheriff Mangat winked. I faked a smile and wished the officers well. As they headed to the squad car, Sheriff Mangat snatched the notebook from Deputy Larson's hand and began an argument with an accusatory finger.

As I entered, my back immediately flew to the door and stomach acid flooded up to my pharynx. The eyes of the townsfolk upon me, judging as guilty, even though I was innocent, or so I believed. I dashed to the staff restroom, flung open the stall door, and expelled every ounce of Thanksgiving dinner. The ordeal lasted for three minutes, the acid corroded my throat and made my breath hot. After flushing the toilet for the sixth time, I went to the sink and washed my mouth out. The acrid taste of semi-digested turkey and baked Macaroni and cheese, collard greens, cranberry sauce, and sugared ham lingered I decided to opt out of Grandma's stuffing, for it had been frozen since last Thanksgiving.

I stared at my reflection for far too long, wholly unaware of who I was. Bezel or Natalie? I didn't have an answer at the time, but what I did know was Malach was not missing but rather acting. The coroner was the offering for the ritual…and Miranda Marshalls would serve as host. I also knew that if he went through with it, his fate would be sealed. *I had to stop Malach from completing this dark sacrament.*

I came to my senses during the last seven minutes of my shift (seven because my mom says I never do things halfway). By this time, I'd finished tidying up the shelves, attended to the perennials, trimmed any overgrown roots, and swept away pints of soil that spilled from a minor miscalculation in bag-to-pot distance. These basic tasks helped me cope, for my day was spent mentally formulating a strategy. Of which I made very little progress; however, the sublime view of the sun casting through the afternoon haze gave me enough inspiration to continue plotting.

Stray civilians populated the streets this evening; usually there were tractors carrying hay and children around the neighborhoods, pumpkin patches full of couples and families. But because of the murder, and the subsequent missing persons, the community set a personal curfew. Their absence I welcomed openly; however, my heart felt nothing but sheer pity for the Marshalls family.

Although I had not known them in my youth, the Marshalls must have attended the same games that my parents did-how different could they have been from my own? Both families were burdened with burying a child, however, my parents never experienced the grief of an *empty grave*. A sorrowful tragedy, without a proper funeral it became impossible for the family to gain post-mortem closure. I wondered of the wake, and would it still happen. *Doesn't matter if they have a body, the casket's closed.*

Underneath my agony, there was a deeper confliction lying within the bowels of my spirit: *Malach was to blame.* Could I fault him though? Wasn't this for advancement of our craft? Were we not charged with spreading the word of Saturn to others, and what better way than casting a spell, and documenting the process. If tasked with robbing a grave, dare say I could undertake it with proper preparation. Malach was not acting morally, but logically. Instead of waiting for the body to be buried, he made a swift steal from the morgue. And…he managed to obtain his sacrifice in the process.

The town's stereo speaker rang throughout the streets, signaling the end of the six o'clock hour. A guitar strummed while a set of militant snares clapped. With haste, I closed the shop and hurried to Malach's apartment, hoping that Sheriff Mangat hadn't beaten me there. As I jogged through main street to my car, the community stereo speaker screeched, and the country melody was replaced with a low shrill.

The noise wasn't jarring or earsplitting as one would imagine, rather a perpetual whine that unknowingly dug itself into the cells of the cochlea. Electrified shards of static ran through my skin and sweat leaked from my pores. I could still hear the sound even as I turned up the radio in the vehicle; music wasn't in my interest, but this shriek was maddening and my spirit longed to be deconstructed and examined like a dissected cadaver. Finally the apologetic voice of Mrs. Janice broke the haze and she blamed it on a technical difficulty.

Her confession was to my relief. I hadn't known if the sound was external…or internal. It sounded like a distant cry from another dimension…incomprehensible lyrics that tickled my ear. But during that droning shrill, originating from a sentient entity no doubt, I briefly thought I heard the voice of my brother, Victor.

I arrived at Malach's complex with no delay and was relieved to find no police vehicles in the vicinity. Parking my mother's car in the lot I reached his room in an instant (being on the first floor was an advantage). The door was locked, but I didn't even consider knocking; instead, I slipped the key out from under the potted azaleas lining his porch and invited myself into the home.

The place was bleak save for a yellow light pulsing from Malach's bedroom. As I fumbled through the dark, my hand scraped a jagged piece of wood randomly positioned in the kitchen. Leading with my good hand, I moved along the wall until found the light switch, next to the microwave. Flipping it on, I was shocked at what my eyes witnessed.

The oddly placed wood that splintered my hand was a leg of the dining room table, broken into jagged boards. Everything in the apartment was destroyed. Smashed by some blunt force object, a large hammer perhaps. Desperately I called for Malach, but my voice echoed like it would in a crypt; the neighbor above banged thrice much to my shock. Creeping into his room once more, I noticed his computer monitor was the source of the light.

Where the living room was a tornado, the bedroom was a beach front after a category four hurricane; everything was in pieces. The camera smashed to pieces, the owl's wings torn asunder with feathers scattered; his bed was folded and broken like a deer hit by an eighteen-wheeler. There was also a pungent aroma in the air…like gasoline.

As I advanced through the wreckage, I realized the computer was the only thing that survived. The screensaver rotated through stock photos until something appeared on the display. A photograph from our first alchemical experiment-we brewed a potion that made one remain conscious during their dreams. How happy we had been…before *it* arrived.

Finding no visible sign of Malach, I left with haste; if the officers happened to make a house call, I'd have no explanation for my intrusion. Presently, the involvement of law enforcement was problematic, for men in uniform are too grounded in reality to understand the astral world, and what powers exist beyond humanity's grasp. Truthfully, they'd probably end up dead or insane if they became too involved, which seemed to be the fate of everybody thus far. *Except me.* The spare key was placed under the mat, and I hurried to the car before any nosey neighbor noticed.

With nowhere else to turn, I chose to regroup at my home, and I planned to call you. My plan was ruined, and I was out of options. Not only had I been unsuccessful at putting an end to Malach's reckless scheme, but the tome was missing too. However, moments before we made contact I received an email from Malach. The document was wordless; the only thing it contained was an attached mp4 file labeled "*Nox Eternis.*"

Curiosity compelled me to open the e-mail and watch the video which was dated Thanksgiving Day. The display blinked twice, and the movie player appeared on the computer monitor. I took a deep breath and tightened my back, bracing for whatever sight I, alone, was about to witness.

II

The first image that graced my eyes was Malach's face; whatever disease causing his body to decompose seemed to be cured, and there was even a hint of redness in his cheeks. Had he come to his senses? I am aware that was a foolish thought, but I needed hope at a time like this. Again he was shirtless, exposing the two-day old runic carvings. Sitting on his finger was the peculiar ring from the container with the feather and needle.

"Father, it is time," were the only words spoken throughout the entirety of the video. He backed away from the camera, establishing his location. I

recognized the cold steel drawers and chalky green walls of the county morgue-we occasionally conducted our meetings in the basement.

Bound and gagged inside the transmutation circle scrawled was a mid-fifties gentleman severely bleeding from his head; part of his hair had been recently shaven. *The missing coroner*. Even though his chest was slowly rising and falling, I knew that death was imminent. Strapped to the back of the very frightened coroner was the decomposing corpse of Miranda Marshalls.

The ingredients I previously procured were ground inside a mortar and pestle until the vegetation became a thick paste. Malach mixed more of the coroner's blood, a strip of Marshalls skin, and his own saliva into the alchemical potion. Then, he drank the potion in one swallow. With all the conditions fulfilled, and his astral abilities greatly enhanced by whatever concoction he created, Malach was finally ready to commit the impossible: *Reanimation*.

Any individual who dabbles in mystical forces understands that to receive, one must first offer something of equal value; to restore a soul, one must be given. Trading the life of another human for power seemed out of my realm of possibilities. However, the same could not be said for my dear friend. Guilt rendered me defenseless as I witnessed sights so horrific they may taint the rest of my memories. Miranda's original face may have been ugly, but the level of destruction and decomposition to Miranda's face was grotesque. It appeared as if a necrotizing bacterium had been released, tearing through the cellular matrix and connective membranes of her rotting skin. Instantly I thought of Victor's boyish face, mangled and burned away by the point-blank pistol. The fate of the coroner was equally scarring; true to my assumption, he was the sacrifice.

Malach used one of the scalpels to slit the carotid arteries and drain the blood in a basin. He drenched the circle as well as Miranda Marshalls with the fresh blood. Then he sliced into the base of the coroner's skull. He had the steady hands of any general surgeon even though he only served as a diener; I wondered if he'd ever cut a living body before? I could not stomach all of it, and yet my mouse stayed put. An unknown emotion held my spirit hostage and I remained fully attentive while the gruesome footage played. What is our fascination with the anatomy, and the occasional dismemberment, of the human body? Eventually, after minutes of meticulous sawing through skull bones, Malach removed *the hippocampus* from the coroner's brain and placed it in the rancid head of Marshalls.

Usually, a magician must chant a specific set of words or perform a distinct action in order to channel astral energies; however, this spell was far from common. There were no mutterings, no excessive shouts or even deliberate movements for that matter. Malach remained perfectly still, eyes locked on the disfigured face of Miranda while his hand pressed against the book. This deadlock continued for another minute or so, and I feared that Malach's lifeforce may have been drained instead of the soul of the coroner. And then he snapped forward, as if whipped by an iron tipped rope.

Suddenly, the gem on his finger shined, and the hue changed from gray to amethyst; a wry grin appeared upon Malach's face as he lifted the device from the tripod.

The lens focused on the corpse's left face-the right side had been annihilated by the hammer. Something slithered underneath her eyelid. It only turned out to be a maggot which burrowed its way back into the bloody mess. The maggot however was expelled from the gaping hole in Miranda's face. An immense terror eviscerated my bowels when I realized the body had moved on its own. The camera then zoomed on her remaining eye, writhing like electrons spinning around a nucleus; the corpse was physically exhibiting a state of REM-like dreaming. Something that can only be done by a living being.

The camera was cut off shortly after capturing the sight; once again, I was left feeling utterly helpless with a black screen and unanswered questions. I immediately decided to contacted you.

"And thus, Grand Wizard…

III

"…This is the end of my tale. If I seemed shaken at the beginning of our conversation, it's because I had only witnessed this clip minutes before," Bezel apologizes over the web camera.

The Grand Wizard taps his index finger upon his sweating temple. After hearing the entirety of her tale, the middle-aged man is visibly shaken. "Was the spell a success?"

"I don't know. That's all I was able to see. And I can't find the file on my computer anymore, or I'd send it to you."

"There is no need, I trust your judgment."

"Grand Wizard, what shall we do?"

Roth stays quiet, rubbing the side of his forehead. "We must meet in person," he finally answers.

"But where?"

"I am in Wichita."

"That's only an hour away, I can get there."

"Tonight?" Bezel nods in agreement, and the silver-eyed man closes his eyes and exhales a deep breath. "I will send you the address. Come quickly and quietly."

"Oh thank you! Thank you Grand Wizard, I shall come at once. Surely with your aid there is no doubt that we can save Mala-"

Suddenly, a deafening screech erupts from the computer speakers and Bezel falls out of her desk chair. The screen flashes bright red and instantly disconnects. She regains her composure in her bedroom, readjusting the chair and keyboard. After settling her nerves, Bezel attempts to call the Grand Wizard. The first two calls fail, but on the third she finally connects.

"What just happened!?" Bezel inquires.

"Something happened to his apartment. An explosion, I think."

"You don't think Malach intentionally...? Wait, the gasoline."

"The fastest way to destroy evidence is to burn it," the Grand Wizard states. Outside of her window, Bezel listens to the faint sirens of the Lindsborg Fire Station gearing up to respond to the disturbance. While staring at the computer display, she notices something off about the Grand Wizard's feed. There is a slight glitch in the display, causing a dissonance between his lips and the audio-it started when Malach abandoned his webcam. Something shifts out of focus; the Grand Wizard has company.

The guest does not yet alert their presence; but it moves a second time. It can't be Malach, right? There's no way Malach could have reached Wichita that quick, or could he? Perhaps the book has the power to grant instantaneous travel to locations previously visited by the caster?

"My apprentice may be rebelling, but he is innovative. After punishing him I will commend him on his resource-By the...what is this infernal..." One of the bookshelves in Roth's room is toppled. In a darting second, the computer monitor crashes to the ground. The webcam remains positioned on the feeble man, who also fell with the bookshelf.

"Grand Wizard! Grand Wizard, what's happening? Roth, answer me!"

"No…stay away…stay away!" His voice is but an echo. The Grand Wizard reaches for the keyboard and slams it against the intruder multiple times.

Finally, a fetid hand breaks into the video feed and snatches Roth's arm with the speed of a cobra strike. An ear-piercing scream wails from Roth's microphone. Blood squirts across the monitor and neighboring walls as the reanimated corpse of Miranda Marshalls snaps the forearm like a dried twig.

The bones pierce Roth's skin, revealing hardened marrow and nervous tissue. The corpse then proceeds to repeatedly beat the man with its bare fist. The pounding never relents, for the golem had no notion of fatigue or mercy. Gore from the face splatters across the volume of textbooks once adorning the Grand Wizard's makeshift office. Judging by the amount of trauma to the head, the false prophet is dead. Despite Roth taking his final breath, it does not halt the corpse from continuing its pummeling.

With no end of the torture in sight, Bezel exits out of her webcam and powers down her monitor. However, what happens now? The spell was a success…and Malach sent the creature over to the Grand Wizard's home…to kill him. It's the only logical explanation for the corpse appearing in Wichita. Now her only possible ally is a pulverized mess of flesh and unrealized dreams.

Tears stream down her face as she bawls out of desperation, out of acceptance and finality. Left completely defeated and traumatized, Bezel crawls into her bed, crying throughout the Black Friday twilight. Although she cries until sleep overcomes her sobs, not a single tear is shed for her brother, Victor.

Vier

*N*ox Eternis...

The haunting phrase stalks her dreams. Nightmares of faceless ghouls materialize within the realm of sleep; Bezel is awakened with a sharp jerk of her legs. Her panting is loud and fast, and she attempts to calm down by lying perfectly still in the abysmal darkness, mimicking the dead. She reaches for a sweater thrown on her wooden stool next to the bed, and heads to the restroom. Each step into the hallway is another curse muttered from the floorboards. Built in the mid-1850's by her ancestors, the two-story home owned by her parents is highly susceptible to creaks and groans, and the occasional growl, especially during the autumn ("spicy days, shivering nights," her mother cackles). After relieving her bladder, and drowsiness, she approaches her desk instead of heading directly to the bed.

Could Nox Eternis be the title of the tome? It's a slim possibility, but it is also the only shared detail between the stories online and her own tragic situation. Although her search is based on an assumption, she still opens her web browser to the Glass Dungeon. Bezel combs through every link related to a search on Nox Eternis. Finally, after suffering countless setbacks, she has a breakthrough; deep within the recesses of the Glass Dungeon, she uncovers an article written in Igbo with a section full translated into English.

At present we have little information regarding the origin of Nox Eternis, and what knowledge we have gathered is miniscule; however, it is enough to share. Not for my own sake, my fate is sealed; but, I share this for the sake of those who may one day find themselves possessed by the book (it's impossible for a mere human to claim mastery over the tome). How this book came into existence is unimportant, what matters is that it exists. Humanity's first recorded incident was on a stone tablet etched with Elder Futhark (pre-Germanic runes) recovered from the base of the Atlantic Ocean, near the northeastern coast of Africa.

Tales of Nox Eternis are documented throughout man's brief stint, however its theorized that multiple incidents remain unclassified (for none are alive to report) or falsely recorded. From incessant research I've compiled a list of potential occurrences indirectly influenced by the infernal tome. As imagined, most are catastrophes: the eruption of Mount Vesuvius and subsequent suffocation, by hot ash, of 16,000 Romans; onset of the Bubonic plague in the Moorish Dark Ages, wiping out approximately 60% of the world's population; on smaller scales there are unexplained mass disappearances, like the Anjikuni in the Yukon territory, or the Roanoke colony from colonial North America (apparently, they were engulfed by a "tear in the sky"; I believe this tear is a portal used to cross the Schism).

The Nox Eternis has also "chosen" certain individuals who possess a worthy will. But often, these individuals are free from the grip of morality; once adorned with this terrible power, they commit heinous atrocities in the interest of the self. A high-ranking SS official who believed in time travel crafted a spell to extract the "lifeforce" of concentration camp prisoners, and used the energy to disrupt the temporal stream; there was a jealous lover who blessed her lascivious husband (a Mongol horse breeder) with immortality, but bound his arms to his legs and cursed him to live out his days in the Siberian wilderness; another, a Danish slave trader tapped into the power of Nox Eternis to indoctrinate my ancestors-the proud West African tribes were captured, eventually giving rise to the Transatlantic Slave Trade.

The antediluvian relic has no author, rather it's suspected that each owner-always temporary-drafts a spell unique to them. It's understood that Nox Eternis has the power to manifest the will of its current holder, and in turn, confine their desires into action, no matter how implausible it may seem to us. Blank pages are the book's defense mechanism, preventing any wandering eyes from gazing at the sacred text. Only those chosen by the book, and those who offer blood, are granted the ability to translate the cosmic lexicon. And then there is the matter of the teeth. Unfortunately, there are only assumptions regarding this, and even they are too far stretched to be considered valid; it's understood that to access the power of Nox Eternis, a source of energy is required. Apparently other body parts have been offered in the past, but the tooth happens to be the best-potentially due to the high concentration of chemical elements within them. Perhaps, one will uncover the true nature of this...however, it seems the books prefer fresh dentition.

I am unsure if this address will be read, but to whomever needs this, do not sign it. Do not...do what I have done. Man is so affixed by his own mortality that he'd willingly run to death if it meant gaining answers. I…have them, I have certainty about everything, but now, I am alone.

Bezel logs off the computer and wipes her chapped lips with menthol balm. All this information, however great it was for her curious mind, is ultimately useless because the book is nowhere to be found, along with her partner. She retrieves a partially crumpled box of Newport from the desk drawer and a tan lighter. Crawling back into bed, she sparks the thin cigarette and draws the curtain. Bezel pulls the black sash across the railing, to open the window-nicotine has a horrible stench.

The first inhale pulls flame and smoke into her mouth, and as she lets the substance settle Bezel glances outside the window, at the backyard. A moonless night, giving rise to a magnificent view of absolute darkness; a chasm where stars drown in the chasm of shadows; the **Void**. The smoke departs her chapped lips and she lowers her gaze.

Light leaks from the toolshed.

Faint and barely visible even amidst the darkness, the luminance pours from under the wooden door. Perhaps her aging father, drunk from one glass of wine, mistakenly forgot to turn off the light when he stored his work tools, but he'd been bedridden all day after eating Grandma's stuffing-along with her mother. As children, Victor and she would escape into the structure-jokingly, he referred to it as a "safe house for sinners". However, Bezel has yet to set foot in the shed again since his suicide, twelve years ago.

She closes the curtain, but the faint light bleeds through the charcoal colored fabric; the cursed lantern returning to plague her sanity. Memories swell like tumultuous waves at twilight and through the haze of thoughts. Her imagination creates a mosaic of images: The damp grass that helplessly clung to her bare ankles, the weight of her father's grief suddenly colliding with her adolescent frame, that unbridled curiosity that caused her to advance inside the shed. And then, discovering the dead body. A permanent scar remembered with lucidity, to the point that even the miniscule detail-like the wattage of the emergency lamp-is an eternal blemish on her mind. Haunted by the sight of a near headless body that once had been called friend. Student. Son.

Brother.

The curtain opens again, the light flickers gently in the calm twilight. If she does nothing the light will eventually extinguish, and she'd be able to conduct a thorough examination in the morning-sleeping would hasten the process. But this couldn't wait. Shaking her head, Bezel leaves the bedroom. Despite knowing nothing good can come from the haunted lantern, she needs to know what has taken refuge and desecrated the site of Victor's death.

Wearing her father's boots (they were the closest pair to the back door), Bezel steps outside. The night gust coming from the west awakens every cell in her body. Before approaching the entrance of the shed, she dips around back and snatches a three-foot wooden stick mainly used for keeping critters at bay-it's a better weapon compared to her fists. Exhausted eyes stare upon the wooden construct like a freshly departed soul gazing at the fiery gates of Hell. Chippings from the previous paint coat are exposed on the shed door and there is a small hole in the bottom right corner, a crawlspace for mice.

Oh, if only this whole ordeal could be explained by a lost rat. A bloated, dead rat with a stake impaled in its heart.

She presses her hand against the splintered wood and a terrorizing dread halts her progress; the air in her lungs expels upon the onset of a momentary panic attack. Flashes of Roth's brutal murder, the surgical excision of Malach's tooth, Miranda's shifting eyelids, Victor's blasted jaw; each graphic image replays in her head on hi-res. If her fate is to die by this abomination, then she wished she'd chosen a better outfit-an oversized wool sweater and her father's boots.

The door lurches open, creaking like a ghost galleon.

The flickering light momentarily blinds her. Everything inside is the same as it had been twelve years ago, even the bleach stains on the floorboards-her father had tried to scrub away the blood. On her left is the shelf hoisting farming instruments: wide-head shovels, shears for the hedges, spare lawnmower blades and diesel fuel; the right contains a handful of power tools, including her father's rusted chainsaw. Bezel rubs her finger against the oiled machine and pictures herself hacking through creatures as if she were Ash from *"Evil Dead"* but the imaginary deadites eventually turn into the headless ghouls that curse her dreams. And then the ghoul transforms into the decaying corpse that attacked Roth; now, the chainsaw is hacking through the reanimated golem.

The shelf suddenly rocks and a bag of nails spills to the floor; Bezel nearly knocks the chainsaw from its post. She is about to swing the stick but the sight in front of her transmutes her frustration into faith. "*Malach,*" she cries.

Laying underneath a greased towel is her partner. With the lantern broken, it is too dark for her to accurately recognize his features, but she undoubtedly knows it's him. At first, she thought him dead, as he remains unresponsive to her inquiry. Upon her touch, Malach spazzes and curls into a fetal position. An agonizing wheeze escapes his lips caked with dried suppuration. Bezel drops to his side, joyful and sorrowful tears streaming down her face, and cradles him as a grandmother does when putting a crying child to sleep. Low sobs and heart-aching gasps drain from Malach's mouth as he clutches the sleeve of her sweater burying his head into her chest.

After bringing the disheveled Malach into her bedroom, Bezel evaluates the status of the Midwestern magician of the macabre. Pale, whitecapped peaks with pulsing red sores blister across his flesh; his finger adorned with the mysterious ring is blackened-most likely from gangrene. However, the most apparent (and shocking) change was his eyes. When open, which became an arduous ordeal for him, the pupils were dilated. Hollow and abandoned, as if the soul lighting his life was snuffed out. The once hazel iris deteriorated, leaving his sclera severely cyanotic and ready to leak out of the corners of his eye socket.

She gently positions him across her patterned comforter. "The first time I get you in my bed, and you're like this," Bezel nervously jokes. Raising his head to sip the water that she'd poured in a tall glass, Malach forces a faint smile; the missing incisor serves as a reminder of his deeds.

"Thank you."

"Don't thank me," she whispers. Emotions flare through her cheeks.

"No, I must. Thank you. Can I be polite, please?"

"Enough, politeness doesn't fit you."

"Fine," Malach coughed. "What does fit me?"

"*Idiot,* for starters. But I won't beat a dead horse. What's done is done, right…Nicolas?"

He gawks at her momentarily before chuckling. Although near inseparable since their initial introduction, Malach never revealed his birth name to her. When one underwent the Septum trials, to earn the rank of neo-necromancer, they shed everything, including their earthly names, earning instead astral identities that, supposedly, originated from Saturn. "So…you know who I am."

"I do. The police came by the other day, asking about you. They told me your name there."

"Ah, I guess there's no point in hiding behind this fake name anymore, seeing as I have limited time. But you…Natalie…you have time." The ceiling groans in her room; gradually, the darkness dissipates as the dawn arrives. "I'm sorry Bezel, I never shared it before. I…I don't know if I can live under that name anymore."

"Stop that, you are who you are, regardless of your name. And call me Natalie, at least for tonight."

"I confess, I prefer you as Bezel. Not that Natalie isn't pretty."

"It's a pretty name for a pretty girl with a pretty life; but me, *I am a magician*. However, just pretend I'm a pretty girl, only for tonight."

Malach reaches forward to hold her hand but retracts it before contact is made; he coughs up blood. "Sorry, what were you saying?" A few droplets land on the comforter and she immediately cleans it up.

"It's…it's not important. No more apologies either. In fact, no manners. Ew, if Nicholas is this polite then I don't want to know him. Bring back Malach."

"Ha, Nicholas is far from polite. But Bez- I mean Natalie, I fear that I am no longer Nicholas or Malach. I…I don't know who I am. Or if I was anything at all. The things that I've done…"

"Stop."

"The Grand Wizard…my quest for power led me to self-mutilation."

"Nicholas, rest."

"I stole a body from the morgue; killed the coroner, and the Grand Wizard. He wasn't even useful. Why did I take his life? To prove that I could do it? That I had dominion over life and death? To appease my envy? Was it worth it…? No."

"Nicholas, cut it!"

His temperament elevates to heights that Bezel has yet to witness-she's also afraid his shouting will awaken her parents. "WHAT HAVE I EARNED MYSELF BUT THE BANISHMENT OF THE SOUL! I

SACRIFICED MY SPIRIT JUST TO...just to...to apologize." Malach's screams turn to sobs, "That's it. That's all I wanted, I missed him. I wanted to talk with my father again. But instead....instead I have become a heretic. One with no regard for death! I am truly the horr-"

A thundering slap cuts across the man's left cheek.

Nicholas massages the site of impact on his face. "I'm sorry, but I had to. Please, your voice. I'd rather not have to explain any of this to my folk," Natalie gasps. "Not like I'd even know where to begin."

"I'd say sorry, but apparently that doesn't fit."

"This is an exception, idiot." Natalie tosses the eraser on her desk at Nicholas, the object clocks him in the head, and they both share a brief laugh before it is suffocated by the impending doom. An uncomfortable silence follows. Natalie toggles with the mouse on her desk. The display glows illusory gray like the library painting of the tumultuous sea-waves at the mercy of forces beyond their comprehension. She resumes her internet browsing while Nicholas reclines against the bed; his swollen eyes concentrate on the lustrous jewel on the ring. Now the color is magenta as opposed to charcoal as it had been when she first saw it in the cover.

Natalie's thin shoulders tense, "Do you still hear the whispers, what do they sound like?"

"Gone. I haven't heard them since Thursday, when I completed the ritual...They sounded familiar. It resembled the voice of my father, as if he were shouting from a deep well and only I could hear the cry. That's why I did it...why I brought her back. I wanted to develop a rejuvenation spell and use it again, this time on a proper host. This was supposed to be an experiment...a trial. Is that so wrong of me, to invoke evil in the pursuit of empirical data? If this succeeded...then I was going to bring *him* back." Bezel tucks her lip between her teeth to hold back tears; Nicholas's labored breathing alters the pace of the conversation.

"Who is him? You mean...your father? Nicholas I..."

"*I pray whatever is inside that corpse isn't him.*" Nicholas tries to twist the ring off, but his blackened finger is swollen. He decides to add more force to the yank; shards of pain passed from his palm to the shoulder. A pop echoes.

"What was that noise?" Natalie inquires, turning away from her screen.

Nicholas curls his hand into his chest. "I...never mind. What are you searching?" he diverts.

"I don't even know anymore. I've been trying to find anything or anyone to help us. I've checked nearly everywhere on the Glass Dungeon, but I hope there is..."

"There is nothing to hope for. No help, no aid, no answers."

"How do you know? I may know more than you realize, such as the title."

"A title will not aid us now, not since the spell is still active."

Frustrated, she wheels around in her desk chair, rambling about searching for remedies, until she blurts out, "Oh hell!" while at the computer. Nicholas raises his body to view the screen, but his spine aches like a needle had been driven through each vertebral disc. "What is it?"

"Miranda's body…it's back in Lindsborg."

"How do you know?"

"There's footage on the news. *Someone recorded it.*"

The morning six o'clock banner flashes on the screen. "A teenage couple found what appears to be the body of the recently deceased local woman, Miranda Marshalls. The body has been missing from the Lindsborg morgue, along with Kane Labe, the county coroner. And…Nicholas Thomas, " Natalie recites the article.

The screen tilts, granting Nicholas a halfway decent view of the display- better than relying solely on his auditory senses. The video feed buffers. Seconds later, the play button appears, and Natalie drags the media player to make it full screen.

The subpar cellphone quality combined with the jerking motions of the videographer made the entire clip a headache-inducing experience. However, true to the anchor's report, the cinematographer captured the body. It was aimlessly laid out on the steps of an apartment complex that recently suffered a fire (Malach whimpered at the sight of his demolished residence).

There are some sights that remain in the memory eternally; unfortunately, for any informed citizen of Lindsborg, which was the entire town, this was one of them. Throughout most of the video the corpse remained stiff, but during the final seven seconds, its arm jerked, dragging the body forward along the sidewalk. Over a week dead, decomposition and the festering mortal wound to the front skull made this corpse grotesque beyond words, and spoiled innards left a trail along the sidewalk. How far exactly had the creature crawled?

The video lasted only twenty seconds, but it was enough time taint the television and imagination. Natalie angrily comments, "How could they show that? Really, how could they plaster another tragedy twisted into a narrative, complete with the gory details that humans secretly love?"

Bezel continues to read the article. "Authorities were dispatched to the location but were unsuccessful in finding any evidence of the remains when they arrived. Some think this to be a prank or a set of hijinks by bored high schoolers, but others are calling it a serious case of grave robbing." Sheriff Mangat and his notebook wielding sidekick appear on the screen at a press conference held in the community center. "Just a week ago, this residential complex was burned down in a fire. One person was killed, another critically injured. Authorities are investigating a possible connection between these two events but have yet to release any information to the public."

Natalie finishes reading the post, and locks eyes with Nicholas.

"It's still animated..."

"I know. I can't explain it, but I feel it. We're bound together; wholly conscience of its anguish and suffering. The body may be dead, but whatever soul occupies the corpse is tortured. And I'm the judicator who's *condemned* them to this harrowing unrest."

"Do not continue to blame yourself, it solves nothing. You chose right, things just got out of hand. So right now, we have to find a way to get them back to normal." Even though she speaks with brevity, Natalie's voice is ready to crack at any given second. She takes Nicholas's hand in hers, glancing at the blackened finger bent out of joint-only tendons held it in place. "If you're…bonded to this thing. Does that mean you know where it's at?" she inquires.

"Ha, I don't think it works like that. It's not telepathy."

Natalie attempts a flirty laugh, but it felt forced and sloppy. She taps the bed next to her friend-her touch might cause more calamity than comfort. "Where do you think it would go, now that it's no longer at your apartment? The morgue, maybe? Since that's where the ritual was conducted?"

Nicholas states with cold logic, "I think...*the mill*."

"Her spirit may never leave that place," Natalie repeats in a low voice. "Let's go now, before the town wakes up. Everybody is going to be playing

'I Spy the Corpse' if we don't do something soon." Nicholas gestures for Natalie to lift him to his feet. She momentarily pauses and disappears into her closet. "First, I need to change." It'd slipped her mind that she'd only been wearing a sweater and panties the entire time.

Malach's mind prevails yet again, proving to be a reliable foundation for humans; even in his horrid state, Nicholas's rational thinking is at work. It's this same cognitive process that attracted Natalie to him-her level of devotion was more than friendship; love, perhaps? While donning a pair of black cargo pants, Natalie asks a question he'd been waiting on it for the entire night.

"Where is it? The book? *Nox Eternis*."

"I...I destroyed it, with my apartment. I thought a fire would purge everything, and maybe, set me free from this subjugation." Natalie remains silent, unable to decipher her emotions; on one hand the weapon of their damnation is gone, but it might've been the only tool for their salvation as well.

"Let's kill it. Or dismember it. I'm sure if we burn the body or something, it will stop. If there's nothing left to move, then we're fine."

"*We cannot.* I don't know how to put this into words, but it's like my…my soul and her body are…one. Believe me or not, but I think if we kill it...then I'll suffer a fate worse than death."

Natalie returns dressed in her ritual attire: a black cloth robe thrown over a cotton long sleeve. She rests against Nicholas's scabbed legs. Her hand strokes through his hair and a few strands come out with each rake. Nicholas peers out the second story window at the sunrise. Warming rays of light shine through the dried blades of grass, and a few fairy-like insects bounce around the horizon. As she observes her exhausted friend, a near identical scene fills her head. Victor. The boy was a master of meditation. For the first hour of his day, he'd sit absolutely still, ground his spirit, concentrate his breathing to where his body barely responded, and decipher every sensation he was currently experiencing. Even the atmosphere surrounding him altered; Natalie believed that she could grasp the secrets of the universe simply by being in the presence of his aura.

Nicholas wraps his wilted arms around her, "If we must do it, then we do it. I am…ready. Although simple, I have lived a life to be proud of, and whatever regrets I may shoulder will be relieved when I am removed from this name. It's time to put an end to Malach, and the monster he created," he pledges with a fierce determination. The embrace unravels slowly, as if it were the last time they'd share a moment as such. And they understand the magnitude of their situation; both are secretly aware Nicholas will face death within the day, regardless of their resistance.

Funf

The rickety sedan "borrowed" from her mother pulls into the deserted parking lot of the Kanerbort Steel Mill. Bezel wrestles with guilt: she is leading a man to eternal damnation-and not just any man either but the one she probably loves. Like a trained chauffer she hustles from the driver's seat to the passenger side and opens the back door. Curled in the seat is Malach, half-asleep; their drive was relatively smooth, aside from the radio report stating roadblocks were in the talks. Bezel couldn't understand how that would help ("to give the community members a false sense of comfort," was Malach's response). However, they did pass a deputy cruiser patrolling the block around the charred apartment.

The necromancers enter through the service door which bears evidence that it had been forcefully opened. The scent of skunk residue, expired chemicals, and *rotting flesh* radiate throughout the abandoned warehouse. Ancient machines and conveyor belts cover most of the ground floor; a set of stairs led to a second floor that held a small office perched like a guard tower monitoring the rows of abandoned assembly lines. Boarded windows prevent the natural light from illuminating the entire warehouse, but there is enough to see. Heavy, chalky dust blankets everything, preserving the industrial ruins in an antique gray. A trail of thick lines runs from the front entrance to a section in the back, near the lockers.

Bezel carries Malach past a rusted construct. "I wish I would have listened to you," he mutters.

"What do you mean?"

"I shouldn't have gotten involved with it. With the book," he says.

"There is nothing that can be done now. You said so already that you weren't yourself."

Malach coughs from the contaminated air as the two follow the trail of gore and entrails strung across the dry ground, appearing like a flayed python. "Only half-true. I was in control, somewhat. I willingly chose to gain this power."

"Why? You've always been powerful."

"Not enough...I...I wanted to...*raise my father*. Or at least, communicate with him."

As they shuffle through the expansive factory, Bezel listens to his confession. She stares into his eyes; the blood vessels in his sclera have burst, and a viscous, navy liquid coats the entire eye. The ocular injury terrifies Bezel, reminding her of the conspirators behind this tragedy. *The black-eyed ones.* An occasional bat shriek disturbs the air but the only sound worth concentrating on is the pulsing in Malach's neck-the normal rhythm is replaced with an irregular beat.

"Our last talk…ended bad. I said some things…that I regret. Blamed his sickness for our financial situation. Said he cursed me to a pointless life, no education, no mother. Just a morgue. All we knew was death, but my father, he taught me to appreciate the end. To embrace it without revolting. Ha, now that I think about it, he probably inspired me to become a magician. But…"

A crimson droplet leaks from his eye, the tear shimmers like gold dipped in magma. "I knew I was in the wrong when I said those things, and I never apologized. Even when I had the chance…I hesitated. And then, I left to spend my nineteenth birthday…placing a hex…on my father…I cursed him out of spite. And the next day," a stream of the lacrimal lava pours down Malach's cheeks, "he died before I could reverse the curse.

"I just wanted…to tell him that I was sorry, and I…I always loved him. And then, I wanted to...do the same for you...and Victor. To bring him back so you could know closure, that he didn't leave you alone on purpose. Yes…the recordings. The files are on my camera; I wanted you to use them. I recorded the spell, from beginning to the very end, so we could have documentation. So we could finally have proof that necromancy deserves to be at the pinnacle of society. Imagine how our members would react upon seeing this, how the world would react when they learned how to beat death…or so I thought. I realized death is and will always be *our master*, and any attempt to escape its clutches is foolish. Tell me…am I a fool for wanting to live?" Malach concludes his address with the somberness of a eulogy.

Bezel remains quiet, but her heart is in conflict. She empathizes with Malach's ambition. To see Victor again…what lengths she would go to if it were possible. And to think that Malach had taken the necessary steps to make that outcome a potential reality; his ravings and inexplicable actions on the camera was for the pursuit of knowledge and understand. Even at the end of his life, Malach, the Midwestern magician of the macabre, was operating with lucidity and logic.

As the two cut a sharp left around the conveyor belt, Bezel registers something near the locker. A humanoid figure although the frame is disfigured. She stumbles slightly, eyes welling with forgotten feelings; Malach crumbles at the sight of his deeds.

"That's foul. It looks hideous...are you sure it's not dead?"

"*It's not.* Put me down here, and then go retrieve what we need for the ritual," Malach wearily commands. Bezel props him on one of the rusted operating chairs, dust floats into the assembly hall of the condemned mill. "What if it wakes up?" Bezel notices the yellow plastic handle of a pipe wrench buried in the dust. She retrieves the tool and places it in Malach's hand.

"*In case it wakes up.*"

Instead of heading to the exit, she turns to the locker. Out of pure fascination for the macabre, Bezel advances closer to investigate the corpse. This rotting vessel was, somehow, Miranda Marshalls. The same girl who threw the fastest recorded pitch out of any Kansas softball player (a whopping sixty-eight mph); the same girl who gave Bezel her first, and only, grand slam. Also earning her the title of the sole athlete in the county to hit a home run off a pitch from Miranda. It hadn't been enough of an effort to carry her team to win the championship game, but the accomplishment was one of the few memories she cherished from her sporting days-coincidentally, the game happened on the fifth year of Victor's anniversary.

Years passed since she'd seen the hulking figure, and she dared not to let her curiosity tempt her any longer; if there is a way for Miranda to retain humanity, it's within these youthful memories. Bezel rushes out of the service entrance, with decisive swiftness leaving Malach and the reanimated corpse in a deadlock on opposite ends of the rusted factory.

The warm sunlight bathes her face as she crawls out of the iron door, but the tranquil moment is spoiled when she notices a person standing next to her car. *Is it Horace the groundskeeper, or had the police followed her?* The patrol could've tailed them. Apprehensively, she approaches her mother's vehicle, trying to gauge this individual.

Judging by the lithe figure, and the well-placed curves, Bezel assumes it to be a woman, but her choice of outfit is eccentric, very different from typical Lindsborg attire ("denim, cotton, and khaki make the citizen's happy," her mother jokes). The parking lot is vacant, and no purring motors echo in the distance, yet, this woman is too pampered to have simply walked from town-five miles out. The stranger rests against the car, adjusting her makeup with a circular handheld mirror.

"Can I help you?" Bezel inquires.

"Why yes, yes you can," the woman responds while applying a thin coat of silver lipstick.

"I've got a phone if you need to call someone."

"I won't be needing that, although some games to pass the time would be nice. I've no time for idle chit chat today, Natalie."

"How do you…know my name?" Bezel's tone flattens as she glimpses at the handheld mirror, reflecting the face of the woman. *Black eyes.*

The woman closes her make up kit and turns towards Bezel. Her jaw line is thin like the legs of a ballerina, and the tight contours of her cheek bones envelope her face in otherworldly beauty; as if Da Vinci's brush had defined her features; and a smile so blindingly radiant that Bezel became momentarily enthralled by the luster of enamel pearl. But the woman bears the same abysmal eyes, the same black pupils haunting her since the arrival of the tome.

"You…"

"Yes, great to see you again. Unfortunately, I'm here on business this time around."

The woman dusted off her shoulder and approached Bezel, "I'm here for Nicholas, or Malach…or whatever obnoxious title he's given himself."

"Why do you want him?"

"*He owes me.* When he signed that contract for power, he made a deal. To call upon the power of the book requires a strong soul as a source of energy, but his initial offering was unworthy…and rejected. Because he botched the ritual, and unfairly stole my precious astral energy, he is now in my debt. But I don't do debt, so I've decided I'm just going to *take his soul back with me.*"

"His soul…no, you can't have it," Bezel defends. By this point, she's reached the trunk of her car, remaining at a cautious distance from the black-eyed being.

"That's one of my favorite lines. You humans always noisily proclaiming to others what you can and can't have, as if you have any control over anything other than those frail corporeal prisons. Tell me, did you demand a soul before you existed, or was it *properly delivered* to that body of yours?"

Stumped, Bezel chooses to ignore her question, mainly because she has more important matters to attend to-and she has no way of answering it. She looks towards the warehouse and her thoughts turned to Malach; which one of them is safer? The trunk pops and she removes a red gasoline canister, a satchel full of alchemical ingredients procured from the apothecary, and a jar of salt for the transmutation circle.

"Ha, is that salt of Atlas? Haven't seen anybody use that since I terrorized the Gaelic druids. I commend your ingenuity, Natalie."

"The strongest women are rooted in the soil," she responds.

The black eyed being flashes the cocaine smile, "Allow me to assist, for you are missing an essential material."

"And what is that?"

"Would you like to use that as one of your questions?"

"Questions?" Bezel stammers. She then remembers their previous encounter, when the phantom took the form of symmetrical twins. "Yes, what am I missing?"

The black-eyed being stands tall and smirks at Bezel. Her palms lay flat against each other, pupils revolve at a remarkable speed, and strange phonetics are spewed from her mouth-the language similar to what Malach chanted on the recordings.

A formless orb oozing in an otherworldly matter materializes in midair in front of the stranger. She swipes through the sphere twice, sending the globular abyss into fabricated streaks across the parking lot. The fragments meld into one; a portal opens. Her hand then dips into the dimensional hole.

"Dark matter, what a mess," the stranger nonchalantly states.

As she pulls her hand from the pit, Bezel gawks at what has been retrieved.

There in her hand was the tooth-covered grimoire.

Nox Eternis.

"I've translated the pages needed to separate his soul from that grotesque abomination. I'm amazed at the spells you humans choose to craft. Reanimation? What is the fascination with the past? Or is it because your species hasn't solved its mortality problem. I sometimes forget how naive your race is.

"So, go quick, I am expected elsewhere. What will the others (*others…?*) think of me if I show up to the **Void** empty handed?" The woman tickles as if it were coffeehouse banter.

How little Bezel truly knew. In one conversation, the beautiful, black-eyed entity effortlessly deconstructed her reality, reiterating there was known end to the unknown. A fire lit inside her chest: she needed to know who this being was…and more importantly, what was this **Void** being mentioned?

"You and I both know Nicholas's fate, but since you have already signed, I'm giving you the option: Get him to perform the reversal, or I do it. And my way, well…none of us will enjoy my way, just saying. These *will* be your last moments with him. Do with them what you want, I'll be waiting out here for you to finish. Those reanimated corpses tend to get…violent, when you try to put them down." The astral creature draped in human form relaxes her posture on the passenger side of the car and basks in the hazy Kansas sunrise. "Don't you just love payday?" she jokes.

Words were useless at this point. Bezel slowly reaches to take the book from her hand. The appearance is different since the last time she'd seen it: the lubricating liquid that coated the cover is now dried, and the fleshy texture resembles necrotizing gingival tissue. The teeth were rotting and some even cavitated, opening holes within the cementum. Bezel dared not to count, but there are at least twenty on each side of the cover. Nox Eternis had collected them…artifacts of the masters (and victims) to the infernal tome.

As Bezel carries the ritual supplies-including the book-to the service entrance of the mill, the black-eyed being shouts. "Oh, almost forgot, don't try and escape. Or I'll be forced to feed you to my pets." She points towards the top of the warehouse; sitting on the edge was a bird with an expansive wingspan. Its translucent feathers cast an ethereal glow across the roof, and the vermillion pockets of flesh under eyes and neck were startling.

A Pharaoh vulture.

It garbles and caws; from the background erupts a haunting chorus. Bezel scans the mill's roof sighting at least sixteen other vultures are perched around the establishment. Their piercing, red eyes reflect the sunlight as the stranger blows a kiss into the wind. At that moment, Bezel realizes that her only option is to obey, lest they all be condemned together.

|

When reentering the warehouse Bezel nearly confused him for the corpse. He is moments away from death, apparent by his slumped body; his chest barely rises an inch, and bile from his gallbladder leaks out of his mouth. "Malach, please answer. Malach…" she whispers.

A soft grunt escapes his lips, retaining consciousness is becoming a difficult task for him. "Must have fell asleep…" he stares down. Bezel bite her lip; his eyes are gone.

All black.

"Malach, I…" Tell him the truth? About the fate of his soul? Why would I condemn him…But, he must've known the consequences of his cheating, right?

"Natalie. After this is done…*leave Kansas.*"

"Wh…what?"

"You said, you wanted to leave Kansas. When this is done…let's leave," he weakly exhales.

"You idiot," she whimpers before her eyes release a stream of tears. The droplets fall to the dusted floor as she explains to him the finality of their situation. The corpse is still motionless, expelling the occasional grunt. Its skin ashen black and green postulations cover the torso; the tendons loosely held together the marrow of the decaying appendages. The eye once again pulses, but the detail is too miniscule for Bezel to recognize from across the factory.

Saying not a word, Malach positions himself inside of a hastily drawn salt circle and opens the text to the page as instructed by the enigmatic woman. Using the last reserve of his strength, Malach begins to read from the Nox Eternis. As the first word of the chant leaves his mouth, the corpse suddenly gargled.

It's awakening. The corpse tears violently at its surroundings, fetid arms smash against the conveyor belt until a decomposing hand breaks from repeated force. Slops of rotted flesh slink to the floor and Bezel gags. However, before she's able to compose herself, the corpse scrambled to its feet. And then it advances toward them. A beam of light shines through a tiny hole in the upper left window, providing just enough illumination for Bezel to come face-to-face with Miranda Marshalls. Grabbing the wrench, she braces for the incoming attack. Her mind, however, takes her back to a memory shared by the two…

She's back on first base with an oak bat in her hand. The rim of her helmet blocks the sun from blinding her line of sight. Standing nearly fifteen yards away is a young woman winding her arm with one cleat on the pitcher's mound. Natalie closes her eyes, inhales a deep breath of crisp, autumn air, and swung with all her might.

BING!

The bat connects with the pitch, and all of Lindsborg watch as the official State Championship game softball flies over the gate. In disbelief, her teammates on the bases begin their jog; as Natalie loops around the field, Miranda Marshalls stands on the pitcher's mound with a wry smile on her face. *Homerun.*

Bezel brings the head of the pipe wrench across the creature's face, sending the mandible flying to the nearby conveyer belt. The force from the impact is so great Bezel accidentally fractures her right thumb-the adrenaline temporarily numbs the pain. However, her well-timed attack fails to halt the corpse's assault. Using its torso as a battering ram, the creature throws its weight into Bezel.

BANG!

The back of her skull crashes against one of the rusted machines and her vision distorts. In the haze, she sees the creature advance closer, with the edge of its fracture pointed and thirsty for blood. The ghoul dives; misses and its bone stabs the steel machine inches away from Bezel's torso. Before she has time to react, it lunges again; this time the blow connects.

The sharp ulna bone pierces her left leg. Blood squirts onto the dust accompanied by an agonizing scream traveling throughout the abandoned Kanerbort Mill. The gash is deep but luckily avoids any major arteries.

Malach's chanting continues. The shambling corpse then diverts its attention to him, dragging its decayed face through the dirt. Because of his ailing condition, the necromancer is unable to ward off the approaching monstrosity. If he even attempts escape, and discontinued the chanting, then the ritual would fail. And the monster formerly known as Miranda Marshalls would roam the earth indefinitely, with his soul hostage. The jagged bone appears again, ready to strike the softness of his neck.

An arm cuts through the air; Bezel chops down with the wrench. Sharp bone fragments slice Malach's ear, but his vital spots remain safe due to Bezel's last-minute parry.

"...*Aluh, snen, ralom!*" Malach howls with his last bit of energy.

Fueled by the desire to protect her partner-and to bring an end to the terror that oppressed their town-she bashes the creature's shoulder. The scapula dislocates from the joint and eventually slides to the floor, followed by the rest of the arm. Again, the wrench strikes, cracking a rib and smashing the bloated spleen. A frothy, brown liquid gushed out of the punctured abdomen. The juices flew across Bezel's jacket, trembling hands, cheeks, and hair.

The wrench connects one final time. The target: the back of the skull.

The creature topples over Bezel after receiving the denting blow. A gurgle escapes from the creature's half-broken mouth; Bezel's mind goes blank as she listened to the soul shattering cry of Miranda Marshalls.

Cerebral ooze, fetid slime, and a dozen maggots that once sat in the mortal wound spill on her jeans; the stench is so awful that her bowels nearly release after one whiff. Panic settles even as one of the grubs crawls into her pants. Pushing with her weight, Bezel threw the corpse off and tries to stand to her feet, but the injury proves too painful for her to rise without stumbling.

Using her hands as paws, Bezel crawls to Malach whose limp head is hung over the book in his lap. "Please…no. Don't be…"

As she reaches out, Malach jumps to his feet. Hyperventilating and spastically snapping in sharp poses. "I'm so scared. Natalie, I'm so...scared, I'm so...scared, I'm...so..." His eyes open, both presenting a portal to the abyss. From the hollow pits drip tears; pure astral energy, crimson micelles shimmering like a thousand cosmos concentrated in his cornea.

Unable to stop him, Bezel suffers through Malach's self-mutilation. He breaks into a violent seizure as pus drools from his mouth. Several bites came to his wrists, gnawing flesh like a ravenous canine-with the incisor still missing in his upper jaw. His wails of agony bellow in the abandoned mill and may have even reached the Main Street of downtown Lindsborg.

The self-mutilation lasts only a few moments, but it's savage enough to leave Bezel hollow. At last, his disheveled body flops against the floor and a plume of smoke rises to the ceiling.

Malach is dead.

III

As she tries to piece together her reality, the chalky sediments covering the first ancient machines vibrate. Malach's body thumps twice, but then she realizes the book in his lap is the source of the shockwaves. A translucent feather drifts from the above, gliding through the beam of light. Soon a Pharaoh vulture descends from the lone open window and lands on, what appears to be, an arm. An arm belonging to the black-eyed beauty she met outside. Somehow-probably during the combat-she slipped inside.

"Honestly, I expected something more touching. A confession of undying love, or some witty final remark; but I suppose this will do," she snickers.

From behind her run the rambunctious twins draped in their identical outfits. Next to Malach's dead body is the delivery boy, the one who started it all.

"Leave him alone," Bezel screams.

"Oh dear, I don't want this waste. Carbon is useless in the **Void**. It disintegrates quickly, and not worth much. Easily farmed."

The young boy tweaks with Malach's hand until the ring is removed, along with the entire finger. Numb to any more horrific sights Bezel coldly observes the posse at work: The delivery boy carries the dislodged finger to the woman, but one of the twins snatches it out of his hands; the identical boys work together to successfully remove the ring from the dismembered digit before offering the piece of arcane jewelry to the woman.

She gazes at the gem, now an opalescent shade of purple, like an amethyst. "Ah, this should cover the amount of astral energy he borrowed. Seems I'm done here," she states while the boys toss the limp finger around. The nether worldly troupe prepare to exit when Bezel rises to her feet.

"Not yet. I still have one more question," she exhales.

Turning with a sly grin, the woman advances to Bezel, but it is the young boy who engages her in discussion. "You may ask."

"I...I need to know, what is this? What is this book called? Everything went to hell when it arrived. What is it, and why did you give it to us?" she pleads.

The woman raises her index finger, "Technically that's two questions but I'm in a fair mood. You did complete the reversal without delay and handled that...thing." She sneers at the corpse, "Why you? Hmm." The twins glance at each other and cackle.

"I was bored."

"You two channeled astral energies."

"I picked up the disturbance."

"But you're not that special."

"Oh, please don't think that."

The delivery boy brushes the dust away from his outfits. "I simply wanted to meddle in the lives of mortals. It is so mundane in the **Void**, endless stretches spent in a perpetual static, so I decided to deliver my power to one I thought could unlock it. However, it seems it reached the wrong person. *Nox Eternis* is not meant for those who lack a desire to learn. Its secrets are to be savored by sages relentless in the pursuit of the unattainable flame of enlightenment."

"*Nox Eternis*...so that is the title?" Bezel's lips quivered at the mere mutter of the name. She was correct.

"At least, that's what it is referred to as in your current era. In essence, the book is nameless. Like I am now. Arbitrary constructs such as titles do not harbor significance to us." The black-eyed posse answered in unison.

"But we, I, us, whatever you choose to call us, were once like you. Before signing the *Nox Eternis*. Through it, I was able to cross the Schism, and venture into the **Void**. I scarcely remember my fragile human existence, it's probably been eons. Since then, I have worn a new name with each generation. Witch, druid, soothsayer, warlock, medium, shaman, *grand wizard*...the list continues." The black-eyed beauty tips her head towards the entrance of the mill and inhales the noxious air.

The injured girl trembles under the hungering glares of the vultures. Bezel finally asks, *"What is the **Void**?"* but the identical copies laugh, howling like rabid wolves.

"Uh-uh. That's another question."

"And you're all out of tokens."

"She'll make an offering to the book though."

"And the book will accept it."

The delivery boy lackadaisically prances across the grisly scene until he reaches the rotting tome. "Human…Always longing for instant gratification without first considering what is being traded for said gratification. If you wish to know more, if you wish to transcend the realm of man and discover the Void, then you know what must be done."

A feather from the wing of a Pharaoh vulture is plucked and handed to one of the adolescents; the other retrieves a rusted nail from a conveyer belt. In the hands of the delivery boy is the Nox Eternis-congealed in slime.

"But Ma…Nicholas used it and got…" still too soon to put into words.

"Men never take the time to learn before leaping. My power is unlimited, only those wholly dedicated to enlightenment, those with inquisitive wills, may unlock its potential. Obsessed with the discovery of the unknown, revolting against the ignorance that is all too comforting. Natalie…I have watched you. You have inquired in ways that he did not, and the fate he suffered may be avoided, if you dare to accept apprenticeship."

Before she can engage them regarding what happens next, an ear-splitting shrill renders her immobilized by the pressure of the gravitational flux.. From her angle she again witnesses the impossible become real: a fragmentary portal materializes-identical to the one the woman formed when materializing the grimoire. *The Schism*. The beauty enters first, departing with a blown kiss and a wink. The twins scramble across the grounds before leapfrogging their way into the pulsating abyss.

"He who has power may reign as king…"

"…But only those with wisdom rule as gods."

"The choice is *yours*," the delivery boy mutters as he departs through the inorganic portal. Suddenly, the vacuum swallows sound and light as the interdimensional tear dissolve into glimmering particles evaporating in the atmosphere, along with the three Grand Wizards-and probably the evidence of their existence in this town, or in this time.

Bezel rips a piece of her shirt and forms a tourniquet around her leg to prevent any further blood loss. To her left lies the body of Nicholas Thomas, and on the opposing side is the corpse of Miranda Marshalls. As the chill of December crawls into the derelict Kanerbort Steel Mill, Natalie finally accepts her fate. Life had given, and life had taken from her; and, the only thing she has to show for sacrificing the man she loved so dearly is the Nox Eternis.

Epilog

A deafening shriek whistles from the locomotive engine as wheels grind against the steel tracks. The Topeka train station is thriving with energy as the travelers prepare for the incoming new year celebration. An announcement rings over the intercom while passengers move from one side of the station to the next. Most are wearing winter jackets except for a couple sitting near the vending machine-the husband dons a Hawaiian shirt while his wife toys with the ribbon on her brand-new straw fedora.

Sitting on that same handcrafted bench, closer to the departure monitor is a young woman dressed in a cardigan and weatherproof jacket. A pair of polarized sunglasses protect her eyes from any light-or wandering gazes. Next to her is a book bag and a medium-sized suitcase that's seen better days. Curious as a child, the woman reads through the various destinations that slowly appear on the display.

The clerk running the ticket counter offers a genuine Midwestern smile. The wandering woman returns the gesture and approaches the booth. She, however, does not remove her sunglasses.

"Hiya, where you headed for the New Year?"

"I'm actually not sure yet. It's my first time traveling outside of Kansas…and I'm a bit overwhelmed," the woman bashfully confesses.

"First timer you say? I remember that feeling, heading out to some unknown destination with nothing but a bookbag and your britches. And that could be a lot or a little depending on how well you manage baggage space," the clerk jokes.

"Hopefully better than I manage men," The woman responds with a soft chuckle. She then glances at the magnets around the clerk's counter. "There are so many, have you been to all of these places?"

"Believe it or not, I once was considered an adventurers of sorts. I used to run the concessions on the trains before I retired, now I work here part time. My husband was a conductor for twenty-seven years until he got sick; when he couldn't work anymore, I promised I'd always bring a souvenir from wherever I went. First it was mugs but he stained them with coffee, then shot glasses but he lost them in a move, so we settled on magnets.." The woman gently nods. "Magnets are perfect gifts. They sit almost anywhere and are easy to pack. Never get lost either."

Three melodic beats rang out in the station and the announcer buzzes onto the line. Judging by the phonetics and the speed at which the words are said, it can be assumed that it's an older woman behind the microphone. Using her well-tailored tone, the woman provides the traveling citizens with the daily gossip.

The Lindsborg Lion's softball team won the State Championship, and the team unanimously decided to dedicate the trophy to the family of Miranda Marshalls, who was once the star pitcher of the team. While a member of the team, Marshalls had nine no-hit games, and holds the highest pitching average out of any female athlete in the Midwest. Throughout her career, only one player managed to achieve a homerun from her pitch. Marshalls family claims they are forever indebted to the school for providing them with the honor.

"Do you mind if I look at a few? I think I'm going to decide where to go based on which magnet I like the most."

The clerk brightens like the star on the Christmas tree displayed outside of the station, "Oh, why yes!"

The woman examines the souvenirs, tilting her head to peer through the gap of her sunglasses, before pointing to one covered with graphic trees and the image of an airplane. "The city of oaks, I love it. They have a big acorn drop downtown on New Year's Eve." The ticket clerk taps on the keyboard and processes the payment, "You should check it out while there." Using her left-hand the woman tucks her black hair away and is about to put on headphones until the clerk motions her.

"I'll take a *one-way*, please," the woman removes a wad of twenties from the pocket of her jacket and slides it underneath the glass shield.

The clerk accepts the cash; her fingers flip through the bills as she counts the amount. "I must say, I adore your ring. Is it handcrafted? I've been looking for something to buy my daughter for her birthday."

"Oh this…" The woman stretches out her hand and rolls back the sleeve of her burgundy sweater to give the clerk a better view. "It was a gift from a dear friend of mine. Truthfully, I'm not entirely sure where he got it from."

"Sounds like more than a friend; tell him he has great taste. It's beautiful, what kind of stone is that?"

"An amethyst."

"I thought so, that shade of purple is alluring. Thank you, I'll have to keep searching but at least I have an idea of what I'm searching for." The clerk removes the receipt from the printer and hands the receipt, and a pen, to first time traveler. "You know, they say amethysts have the ability to channel a soul, if you believe that sort of thing," the clerk winks. A forced chuckle leaves the woman's mouth as she signs the ticket.

Three more beeps echo throughout the station.

The county morgue caretaker, Nicholas Thomas, and the coroner, Kane Labe, are still considered missing. There was talk that stress from the unchecked workload at the Lindsborg morgue drove Thomas to the edge, and the brutality of the Marshalls case was a tipping point; the apartment belonging to Thomas was burned to the ground on Black Friday. It should also be stated that some of the bodies at the morgue had their teeth stolen. Police are set to investigate this in connection with the Marshalls case, although authorities believe it was foul play. A tip line has been set up, and there is a cash reward for anybody who provides information regarding the disappearance of these two individuals.

"A marvelous signature," The clerk accepts the receipt and passes the credit card, and train tickets, underneath the glass partition.

"My mother says I have the best Handcock in the Northern Hemisphere," she admits.

"Well, she's not wrong about that. I should know, I've seen plenty. Anyways, your train to Raleigh, North Carolina will be loading at station four. You'll make a right down the hallway and continue straight until you see the gate marked on the board. Follow that and then you'll arrive at the tracks. Show this ticket to the conductor and he should let you on with no problems. Now, Ms. Natalie Carson, I could wish for you to have a happy New Year's, or to enjoy your vacation; but you're not doing that. You're going on an adventure, and you don't plan on coming back here for a while. I should know, I've seen plenty. So, I'll tell this to you, as I tell it to all of them, 'home is not a place, it's a person; home is your head.' So when it gets rough, and it will, remember that your mind is a refuge."

"If I happen to return, I'll make sure to bring an amethyst." Natalie promises.

The clerk laughs as she waves off the customer, "Oh honey, I hope to be long gone by the time you return! Now, go!" the clerk shouts, "your train is boarding in twenty-five."

After rummaging through the unzipped hole for a few moments, Natalie exhales a sigh of relief; thankfully, nobody tampered with her stuff.

Natalie cuts her way through the festive station. Around her are beaming faces busy posting statuses about their resolutions and taking selfies with family members who recently arrived from faraway places. The star on the Christmas tree is the highlight of the monolith. During her youth, she and Victor would set aside two hours to help decorate their family tree. She always had the honor of crowning the top with the star-the ritual originally took place on the Saturday after Thanksgiving.

A custodian sweeps around the departure display. Above him, the intercom chimes again, and the elderly gentleman raises his head toward the ceiling to listen to the new announcement.

The body of Miranda Marshalls was finally cremated and returned to her family. Law enforcement have a key suspect in custody. Horace Martin, the groundskeeper of the Kanerbort Steel Mill was arrested and will undergo trial for first-degree murder. According to Sherriff Mangat and Deputy Larson-who made the arrest last Saturday at cribbage-Martin went on a drinking binge after an unsuccessful night at bingo the week of Marshalls disappearance. Horace blamed his bad luck on the moderator, claiming that he was being cheated out by Marshalls. Later that evening, Marshalls was with her girlfriend, Miss Sylvia Maynard, at the bar when the two were verbally assaulted by a few citizens for "expressing their sick love." Horace was one of the rioters, and even became violent, slamming a glass against the counter. He was escorted off the premise, but after the altercation he chose to stalk Marshalls home after the couple split at the library. It was on this walk back that they believed she was assaulted and subsequently murdered by the suspect-some blame the veteran's unchecked PTSD as a motive. Court hearings are to begin in January...

The voice above continues to drone while the custodian collects trash left on the bench. Next to a plastic wrap is a small object. Since he's wearing gloves, he can thoroughly examine the object-as all custodians must do before discarding objects. However, he is baffled at what he holds in his hand. In the twenty-five years he's worked at the Topeka train station, the custodian never found a missing tooth before.

Out of the corner of his right eye-his good eye-he peers at the person last seated at the bench: the woman standing at the Christmas tree. "Ma'am excuse me! Ma'am with the sunglasses," he calls out. A few of the migratory citizens broke from their routes to stare at the minor spectacle, but since vacation is so close, they only pause for a moment. The young woman pivots to greet the elderly custodian, who is short of breath from the light jog. He gasps for air, raises his hands to her, and presents the rotted tooth. "Found this…at your spot…not sure if you'd be wanting…it back."

A pair of fingers lift the missing incisor. A beautifully white smile enthralls the custodian, enamel shimmering like diamonds cast in sunlight.

"Ah, that makes four times successive results. A tooth will be shed three days after a spell has been completed, and the energy depleted. It seems I don't have to power the tome with my own teeth; but the fresher they are, the more energy they contain."

Natalie removes her sunglasses; the custodian drops his mop. Her eyes are hollow, black like the **Void**. The abysmal darkness is present in the sclera; however, there is a hexagonal ring glowing around the pupil. "There is much to learn about you, Nox Eternis. Say," the black-eyed beauty leans forward with a devilish grin, "you wouldn't happen to have any *loose teeth*?"

The Hopeless Home

I am trapped in an abandoned house with the Joker,

his reflection is the form of a man with tattooed
hands (and yes, *love* is this word). Today is the day.
And, what a day, what a glorious day! A dance
in the woods, sun setting over a vast lake as we witnessed
the exorcism of a spirit rooted in soiled souls.
Our very lives, the fabric of this branded
existence, *the dreams after one thousand sleepless
nights* are embedded in this singular moment. As if
the sentinels who guard the hourglass of Midas, momentarily
quit their posts, allowing us thieves draped in inspiration to
rob them, leaving only an oil-soaked feather. Tilting
the world's axis a degree, gripped by the suffocating feeling
parasitically latched onto our golden moment. We
depart the vast lake painted by the sunset, and
the world darkens. Our voyage carries us to *that place*.
The video equipment is hauled from the street
into the woods, traversing a ditch, hills infested
with thick roots, and translucent webs. It came into clear view.
The Hopeless Home
That wretched construct lying in the thicket, decaying,
thirsting for any sentient being with a beating
heart wandering about in the moonless night. A perfect
set for a snuff film. What compelled us three to enter on
that frigid night remains unknown, however, the calling to create
something beautiful in a broken place appeals to the artist.
The front porch was demolished, impassible so we crept
around the back, where a sunken outhouse gloomily observed
our intrusion. Words were exchanged before we begun
but recalling them at this time remains too great
a task. Waiting any longer at the door
would consider us cowards, so we entered.
Upon our initial visit, I knew this home doubled as a crypt.
Which made us nefarious trespassers, bringing self-centered art
to a domain of imminent despair. Who were we to encroach
upon this shambling foundation, as if it were abandoned?

But the home is so cold the dying
Air escaping my pleural cavity becomes
corporeal. Dust from the strange rubbish on the floor
twirled in the flashlight beam as we stepped slowly. It is odd,
the material we stand upon is most bizarre. At first,
one expects to experience the feeling of combat
boot to arid sand; however, our first
journey (a fortnight ago) to this demolished home dispelled
the foolhardy hypothesis. The rubble was soft, gentle
like clouds; but the tarnish far from the graces of
heaven. What an ugly shade of pink
the walls are, peeling chips long untouched
reminiscent of scabs upon the knee. I imagine this
is the residence of a ghost, not of the dead variety,
but the living who decided disappearing is an ideal
alternative to dealing with the world at large. So far
removed from the eyes of a bitter society that milk
cartons are unchanged for there is no hope in discovery.
The Hopeless Home...
I am bound by the principles of Prometheus
to bravely venture into the realm of uncertainty, and
escape with a torch of truth. I pause the brain
and allow fear to ferry me through Styx,
the body becoming a devoted Charon.

-Her voice broke through the shivering darkness-
"What is that on the wall...?"

What wall…?
There should be no wall unfamiliar
to my eye. I recognize these walls for they met
my sight twice-and you know what they say
about the third. We pause, and gawk
at the sight. The Joker asks to break
the mirror; I ignore him for my attention is glued
to the wall, and this note. The letters are illegible
unless one crosses into a risky threshold, choosing

details over safety. We peer at
the parchment carefully positioned
upon the wall; scratches that cannot
be reached by nails, upon my brow
as lips curl to read the
lettering. This phrase alone was enough
to retreat to the uncharted forest
in my mind. I dared not allow
my curiosity the best of my rational thought,
forgoing a magnified view of the
note in the interest of personal safety. Reading
curses can invoke the evil, granting Lovecraftian
unknowns entry into our frail existence.

"God has given us two ears"
-Leaving the note, she suddenly remarks-
"There's another."

This note is bubbly and childish, lazily
drawn on the picnic table in the blood
orange haze of summer; yet this paper is
hung at a height no sapphire-eyed youth can
reach. No, this is the work of an adult. A
hulking ogre with intent to rip my spine from sacrum,
no doubt. Neatly pinned at such a frightening height was the name:
Felicia.
A star decorated the letter, "I".
Pointless whimpers escaped my chapped
lips; the Joker, with makeup smeared on his
face is aware of the situation. The red
sphere blinks in the corner of my camera, serving
as a visual metronome for the madman's soliloquy.
We drones obliged the hive mind of art, risking sanity
for the pursuit of sealed truths. Only hearts have
the power to restrain the anxiety, but…

Who deemed us worthy of fulfilling this hopeless purpose?
We are but guppies waiting to be gulped
by the Leviathan lurking in the abysmal trenches.
What of the owl of Athena, providing conviction
to us, the irrational (or intelligent) intruders of
this derelict residence.
I wonder at the curiosity of the audience, the theater of obscure
faces tasked with interpreting this product.
Will they gather hope when they see this?
Hope has always been the dream
of Man; the belief manifests from a hastily constructed
will, held together by tendons of faith; and I
pray, this is where it takes its last
breath; a final sigh tangible as the icy
whip of apprehension latched upon my neck.
To hope for change is to exist as
an enslaved with knees bound to the ground, and yet…
We experienced a moment of so-
called "hope", and my desire to flee through the broken
window ardently increased. Where was hope? Written
by the hands shrouded in blood and midnight, upon
the wall where the ghastly message had been etched?
It wasn't here with us in the Hopeless Hope.
Bound to rusted chains that obliterated the proud
spirits of my ancestors. How can one aspire
to have hope while strung about
by faceless puppeteers, where the slightest twitch of arthritic
fingers divert the direction of fate? It is inevitable...
The witching hour draws near; and in this cabin
we are trapped in an illusion, unaware of the world outside
these walls. Prisoners to tension and yet passion
dares me to throw my hands in hopes of
pressing forward. Even after using it, I come no closer
to understanding hope, but it has saved me. And
with this conviction, we decide to record the video.

The Joker erupts
in a gritty monologue,
lips curling in the
boreal night, but words
he does not speak.

Indiscriminate slurs,
grave-bound
grunts by writhing
tongues, and poems
transcribed from pain.

He pantomimes; the
pressure of his
spirit sets the room
ablaze; I am
reminded of childhood curses.

The hex has succeeded,
turning my attention away
from reality, tossing my
mind in a gutter of ooze
and corrosive ambition.

My vertebrae reach
the qualms of a surrender,
and the throbbing of my viscera
cannot be contained by elastic veins
alone, so apprehension spills into the artwork.
Each click of the camera shutter fills my eyes
with the entire spectrum of light;
the brilliance so radiant that I forgot
the residence is ravaged. However,
the only emotion summoned is *sorrow*.

Will the floor break,
my foot tossed in some
body-filled basement only to be
pulled under and become
the next stiff addition?

I am the wall,
the very point where the nail
amended to the wrist
upon the back of
Felicia's canvas.

Did I just hear a twig
break under nonexistent
feet of the ogre or is the
blood rushing through
the lacerated jugular?

Maybe the beast breathing
in the thicket, behind the
window in the eastern corner,
will finally ignite
their predatory instincts.

In a flash, he will   See the glorious
moment,
have torn through   the monster with
my abdomen.   snarling teeth,
oh, how foul   seeking the next
to witness this;   kill, appearing in the
dark
                    The splattering
                              organs–they
            say disembowelment
                    is in fashion.

Lying on the soft earth, half the
man I used to be,
I'll observe the striking
quality of its bestial features. The bulbous
nose resembling cliffs above putrid waters,
the ivory bloodlust materialized in pupils;
they reflect the dying light. And its jaw, how shapely
defined as if Michelangelo was commissioned
by the commander of the Ninth Circle and given inspiration
one final time to chisel centuries of undiagnosed violence
and maddening thirst for erythrocytes into this panther-
like mandible. The last thing I may very well see
will be the foamed jaws of the beast of Revelations
hibernating in the home we have invaded.
They say hope is found on the inside,
maybe I will locate it among my distended cecum?
Alas, that was only a noise, and so far,
as modern science has extensively proven,
noises are unable to disfigure a body.
The Joker continues his hysterical rituals;
My camera can no longer predict his movements.
Erratic and spastic as if a queen ant burrowed between ribs;
there she laid ten-thousand eggs, circulating through the four-
chambered dungeon of crimson walls; and,
after being transported to his appendages,
they hatched simultaneously with gnashing fangs.
The golem in front of my lens has condemned me
to this brief instant, altering the flow of the temporal stream,
but only for a moment. We exist as one organism, shared by
two vessels: source and projection.
Providing the darkness with a contract written in
blood, by ink from a snapped quill.

Our video called for an assortment of props:
a series of Frank Sinatra records;
the torso of a jester; wick and spark; a bowl of
packaged fruit waits to be crushed in suffocating fists,
and smeared across a neck and gaped mouth;
and, a marron rose symbolizing the fragility of the end.
But none were as fascinating, and oddly placed, as the mirror.
It was erected in the supposed bedroom in front of a child's sock.
Angled to the chalky walls as a corpse rising from a dark soul
-its appearance utterly enthralling. Mesmerized by the
reflection of this broken foundation, I wept; who knew
beauty could thrive in the hopeless? My friend,
the Joker, who I've shared fond memories with-
by the same tranquil lake at sunset-
has disappeared beneath the finger paint.
In his representation is a spirit bound to a cursed object.
This newly birthed creation is in the corner of a grimy room;
it's possible we may have been in limbo.
When did we barter our souls, was this the unknown
entry fee, the ante required to bet on this moment?
Ah…*the rose* is the source of this revulsion.
The candle in front of the Joker's blackened lips has extinguished,
and I am returned to the real.
Returned to the comfort of light upon my neck.
But there is a fragment of my sanity still locked within that infernal
moment of fear. It makes sense, with the bottle half-empty.
This...this is a blood sacrifice, and I've been deemed worthy
to die in this archaic ritual-since the fall of Jericho,
certain rituals require a living host to face the end with *hope*.
Again, that damn word! How it *pollutes* my mental capacity
for rationality. To lose that would usher the loss of Rand's
individualism, yet it poisons me. Noxious fumes and toxic
particles of chance occurrences travel through my veins,
waiting to sap the divine essence that drives my being.

Why do I continue to have hope in the face
of finality? Do I not feel the searing binds upon my wrist,
the pain yet to rescue me from
this illusion? It is considered depraved to dream
for something so impossible as hope; only the wise
men and alchemist understand its working, and I am neither.
We stole the essence of this establishment,
no longer will it remain anonymous and half-
dead in the dense woodlands. Instead resurrected to complete
a sentence of perpetual suffering-notes strung upon the wall
like strange fruit. To craft this project; we bested the catacombs
of the forested Thanatos and conspired with the phantom warden
to leave a treasure upon our completion-
a strangely courteous act for we were trespassers.
It was the decision of the production team to leave
the mirror for this so-called *Felicia*. If she were a spirit,
this mirror probably had the power to return flesh to her at the
expense of divine currency-*surely, you don't believe such
blasphemy is free*. A mirror...
what will reflection bring to this place?
Will the prisoners of this wooded Hell finally glimpse at God,
reminded of his eternal covenant, the proof burned upon bended
hands when they bear witness to the mirror?
I dare not utter any answers,
for we are still under the derelict roof, but perhaps,
telepathically, I translated my thoughts to the production team.
We changed the status of this house,
this broken foundation clutching tightly to its final rotting beams.
Words evade my tongue, I cannot speak the truth
...not yet.
Now, if our missing hostess happened to retain
a degree of her assigned humanity, then this mirror
will serve as a portal away from pain. In her
reflection, maybe she will find suffering,
because only suffering can invoke

The sublime.

That sense of life imbued with natural energy, a force
beyond the measure of humanity's' greatest inventions;
the ignorant gears will never understand
the magnificence of the cosmos.
Yes, I traveled to this place of dread and infinite
darkness in order to seek something greater than myself,
greater than the entire world that I have come
to comprehend; I sought something that cannot be stated
in any language, only experienced by the faculties that monitor
the mind. The same pursuit of many valiant philosophers
and artisanal thinkers for centuries; do I expect to be the archetype
to quantify it? No, I merely wish to experience this feeling, to be
graced by the sublime at least once in my pitiful life.
I wanted to enter the **Void**.
I apologized again to the home for this vain intrusion,
but rationalize this decision. I have stated time
and time again, until my cords are raw with regret,
that my life has been irrevocably melded
to this moment. Bound like Prometheus; My heart goes
to Sisyphus, perhaps he understands this absurd plight.
Men have always held action higher than the idea, but,
often, unable to project their will into a stable reality. In moments
like this, with terror lurking, we must cling to our fundamental
values, most notably fear of the unknown,
for the unknown must be uncovered. The only guarantee
we humans have is a grave, and even that is uncertain…
few have learned the secrets of immortality.
Is that not what art is?
An immortal conviction of an individual, molded
by the matter of the earth, the energy of both spirit and space,
compartmentalized into tangible inventions that represent the id.
Is that not why we came here? To create.

Hastily, we depart the path
leaving this studio of terror, greeted by the shadowed
thicket. The vines tangle with the tendons of the wilted
branches, gaining momentary animation from Arachne.
We hack with bladed arms until one
final ditch remains. A dried moat that once isolated
this crypt from the rest
of the road-I half expected
the snarling beast to pounce from the shambling roof
and tear me asunder into ribbons of melanin
at the very end. A well-timed step, a
brush of the pine green, the feel of familiar
bark in my hand. Across the moat laid my destination:
Freedom.
Who knew the street was only fifteen-feet away from the front porch?
How splendid the cosmos, how we forget that infinity is always
Inches away; how magic only stopped being real when Man started
answering questions. Was this world not mythical
before modernization? Are we so vain that we subjugate the earth,
and all under its sphere for the sake of self-pleasure? Perhaps…
but perhaps we have found the galaxy
within our own golem, maybe the mystery is under the matrix
of skin and marrow. Then, we can scale our hypothesis
to the homunculus that we call a body, and from it form a theory
to carry us throughout this beautifully short
existence. How quick it moves, like darting comets that glint
for a millisecond, illuminating dots in the
darkness connected by frost-bitten fingers;
and then, it comes to an end…
Like all things.

I remember now,
how it felt when the sensation of raw life strikes
the sorrowful soul, how it inspires even the bleakest.
I raise my head and proclaim with the power of a thousand suns:
"I have hope!"

Mr. Aki-Ki

(On]e

The neon sign lodged within the front windowpane of Parrot Bay, the electronics store, has illuminated the litter-infested sidewalk of my street for the past nine nights. I know this because my apartment-a crummy studio with barred windows, one mattress (no headboard), and a rusted sink-is situated right above the establishment. Each night, after working the graveyard shift, I have returned at dawn to find it lit.

It's odd, the turquoise lights shine brightly, but they are dimming and that worries me. If the parrot has been lit for nine days, then something has happened to her-for the parrot is always turned off when the business is finished.

On day ten, today, I decided to check on my neighbor, Priscilla. Priscilla Douglass arrived roughly three years ago, exiting a taxi decked in a black trench coat with fishnet sleeves and granite jeans scarred by scratches along the shins. *The Matrix* inspired wardrobe was striking and unconventional, attracting judgmental eyes, but she kept to herself during the entire visit. Her mission: to scope out the vacant business lot on the first floor of a twelve-story structure. Priscilla had recently graduated from university with dual degrees in Computer Science and Business; her post-grad plans were to open a used technology store that doubled as a repair station. Two weeks after the initial visit, the space was leased in her name and the neon avian donning a pirate hat became the OPEN sign for Parrot Bay.

The shelves of Parrot Bay were lined with various electronic devices ranging from supercomputer modems, Famicom gaming systems, jailbroken iPhones, home theater stereo systems and wires. Red cable wires to connect landlines, extension cords that could hang from the roof, thick copper cords weighted like an aluminum bat. The digital artifacts were cared for with high regard and were also sold at a higher price range on account of their rarity. However, I also learned that her eclectic collection was not gained without conducting business with jaded figures.

I'm not exactly sure what she did afterhours in that space below my apartment afterhours, but I often witnessed a variety of customers coming at late hours of the evening. Most of them exited with oblong packages or had hooded followers wheeling boxes from the back lot of the store to their vans. By 2:00 AM, when I returned from the late shift, her second-hand business usually reached a conclusion. The store emptied, the neon parrot put to sleep until another shift, and Priscilla at home, conveniently located on the twelfth floor. Except that wasn't the case anymore, seeing as the parrot had yet to power down for the past week.

I returned to my apartment after a grueling shift at the powerplant; the clock read 3:10 A.M. Sleep hit quick as it normally does, but lasted only a moment, as it normally does due to my insomnia. However, tonight I awoke after hearing a quaking from below (my mattress is on the floor). Had Priscilla finally returned? I threw off my comforter and dashed to the window. The unremarkable sight of the neon lights bathed the steel gutter a melancholic blue under the sidewalk. The quaking persisted; erratic and lacking any coherent rhythm or melody. Initially, I thought it was her stereo system, or maybe one of the many televisions in her shop had accidentally animated-occasionally this happened due to the vast surges of energy required to power the store.

I pressed my ear against the tiled floor and listened as the dimming hums transitioned into voices.

Priscilla's voice has a distinct whine, a nasally shrill that she was aware of; she claimed her shyness stemmed from a childhood bout with ankyloglossia which prevented her from talking until six-her parents deemed her mute and "shielded" their daughter from society. By a stroke of luck, a dentist solved the problem during a routine cleaning by cutting the membrane below her tongue; suddenly Priscilla spoke coherently to her parents, causing her father to faint. Although the issue was solved, the social trauma from her formative years prevented her from fully grasping her tone. I share this to say, Priscilla has a recognizable voice. So, I deduced that it was indeed her.

The other, well, it was hard to accurately listen for there were other interfering noises. The quaking hazed with static, but instead of the uniform cracking and rushing sound-like a raging whitewater rapid-it was ominously hollow, as if the source were in some uncharted seaside cove hidden among rotting driftwood and lost bones. Yes, I am aware that eavesdropping is indecent, but you must understand that I had a legitimate reason for my actions. I required Priscilla's assistance as a repairwoman. Try to sympathize, what would you do if your contract worker neglected their duties, and, your neighbor went missing? To the common man, this would've been enough evidence to put concern to rest, but I've been told that Pisces are too empathetic-and my parents happened to consummate their love on a summer evening in June.

For the last nine nights I ventured to the entrance of the store with hopes of retrieving my repaired modem (my game systems often overload the hard drive). Priscilla was nowhere to be found, and hiding is near impossible in a store with quadrilateral windowpanes instead of a brick facade. And on this night, I happened to hear her voice. Company or not, I had to see Priscilla and, if fortunate enough, she'd have my order ready for pick-up.

PARROT BAY

The neon letters hummed like frayed circuits as I peered through the front window. The store was empty, and the overhead bulbs were powered off, enhancing the luminosity of those lights still lit (the neon sign and some other unidentified source in the back office). I tried the handle, but the door was locked, then I tapped the glass with my knuckles, but the echo died somewhere between the entrance and the office. I even called out her name while I was on the street, a dumb move because a nearby tenant verbally assaulted me from the third floor-she dropped at least three "F-bombs".

Again, I scanned the room; waited; pounded the door, even considered picking the lock, but nothing. No response from Priscilla. Something told me-maybe it was the fumes exhuming from the neon lights-that I should've given up, but what of my neighbor's safety? If you can somehow put your authoritative accusations to the side and entreat my confession, then you will soon have the answers. I know this may be hard for you to believe, but I promise…I promise…I'm not in the business of crime; it's a lucrative hustle that only the wisest, or foolish, can handle. So, when I broke into the back door of her shop, situated between the two olive-green, industrial-sized trash bins, I believed my actions to be justified.

I've browsed in Priscilla's shop quite often, no stranger to her wares, but amiss might be an understatement because after finding the circuit breaker, and bringing light to the store, my eyes were met with destruction. Nearly all the television screens positioned on the back shelf had their faces shattered, black and copper wires undulated like pythons constricted in a breeding ball, and various green microchips and computer circuit boards were in fragments on the floor. Naturally, I called out to Priscilla, but not once did she reply; instead, she carried on her conversation with her company. The store was in shambles, and my first thought, just like yours, was a break-in. But why would someone break into an electronic store only to vandalize the merchandise?

I did consider calling help first but a blood curdling cry, followed by a crackling whip, dispelled the idea. Crashing through the office door, I was temporarily disoriented by a flash of light able to rival solar flares. I expected to meet the two silhouettes when my eyes adjusted: Priscilla and her company. However, I only saw one.

Priscilla.

In her hands was a rusted crowbar, presumably the one she kept under her desk-the neighborhood's high crime rate called for "personal security". Around her were more destroyed computer modems and accessories, and it looked as if the final blow had been recently dealt to a 24-inch monitor. The way she wielded her weapon reminded me of that scene from *Berserk* when the cursed warrior just defeated one hundred men, wounded and on the brink of death, yet wholly alive, taken by a primal lust for battle...or *blood*.

Again, must I remind you that Priscilla is the same woman who used the last bit of her savings to procure this place as well as the products that lined its shelves; and here she was, ending the life of every electronic within her reach. However, Priscilla didn't take notice of my entrance or even my presence for that matter; she simply continued her bashing. Shards of the LED screen flew with each downward swing. Rationalizing with her was impossible, no method of communication could quell her rage. But then she flexed her arms like a slugger ready for a fast pitch, or a berserker ready to cleave a crowd of cowards and struck the temple of the television. The glass blew out from the inside and one of the fragments happened to dash across my cheek. A minor cut that I dabbed with my pinky. Before I could dispose of the droplet (either orally or by wiping it on my pants), an apprehension overcame me. I realized that the room had suddenly gone silent.

She stopped so abruptly that. Priscilla had stopped her assault, hovering over the remains like a seasoned hunter snaring the soul of its prey. And then...she stared at me.

With the crowbar tightly gripped.

Maybe it was fear that kept me immobile; the piercing gaze from the berserker; my heart-which experienced a bout of tachycardia at the anticipation of a devastating blow; or the possibility that if I moved, I'd need a new pair of underwear. *Or a new skull.*

Her boots dashed from the shrine, landing not four feet away from me, the cowl of her checkered sweater fluttering like snow behind her. I closed my eyes and foolishly threw my arms up as if they wouldn't shatter upon impact from her strike...but it never came. Instead, she released her other hand-balled into a bleeding fist-and asked me for my phone. I did as instructed, the coward in me had no intention of forming any counterarguments, especially against a friend dazed, and armed. Strangely, she politely accepted the device, laid it on the floor, and smiled at me.

Then the crowbar ascended to the ceiling.

With the strength of the Norse god of thunder, Priscilla brought the iron edge down on my phone screen. The glass exploded, leaving the electronic underbelly exposed. Again, she struck; and again, the phone was further pulverized into pieces. Of course, I wept; wouldn't you if you just watched your digital lifeline get destroyed? After a series of blows, I gave up any notion of salvaging the device or data. However, I was not enraged or angered enough to retaliate, for the threat of death loomed so long as the crowbar was in her grasp.

With the wall against my back and ample space between us, I decided to stay. At first to try and communicate with her, yet she remained silent throughout-disciplined as if completing a direct command from a superior being whose authority over her was absolute. Unable to save her from the illusion, I quietly decided to bear witness to her actions.

Taking the remains of my phone, she set it upon the peak of her makeshift altar and prayed. Then she heaved one of the boxed computer monitors bearing a fatal crack in its screen to the chair. They made little sense at first: tying a few wires around the legs of the chair, propping the crowbar up on the desk, stacking devices atop each other at dangerously sharp angles, and balancing the large computer on the edge of the seat. Then, she went prone on the floor; she muttered a single phrase.

As far as the laws of physics are concerned, gravity will always bring objects down; by the time I realized what her apparatus was, and where she was positioned, Priscilla had already kicked the crowbar. The enlarged modem landed on her face, instantly crushing the bones of her skull while the jagged edges sliced through the adipose deposits in her cheeks (even now, I can still hear that god-awful crunching).

The floor and my outfit were covered in her blood and other fluids; I assumed she died instantly. With the little first aid knowledge I had-my only instructors were actors on reruns of *General Hospital* and other soaps set in a medical field-I checked the woman's pulse.

Nothing. At first, but then her arm shot up. A revolting terror ensnared me when her hand latched onto my shirt. I tried to pull away, but her grip was strong. Shock transfixed my face into a mosaic of melancholy; fear settled in fast when I realized she wasn't dead, but also that it was impossible for her to survive that. Rigor mortis reflexes or not, she would not let go. I eventually had to break one of her fingers to release myself from the grip (a horrendous crunch).

A breathless cackle slipped through the holes in the computer modem as if her spirit had not yet fully fled. It sounded almost like a laugh, an innocent and sheepish giggle that a child would employ when entreated with sweets.

I hastily made my way to the entrance of the office and was about to leave when I remembered the other reason I came here: my order. I then spent the next few minutes tearing away at what remained of the office, shuffling through her desk and filing cabinets. Eventually, underneath the bottom shelf of her closet, I found a box marked "Treasure Chest." Inside were dozens of digital compact discs, each neatly wrapped in a pre-made package. At the top right corner were the names of each of her customers, the patrons who made good use of her exceptional skills as a techie. Why was it called the Treasure Chest, and why was her store called Parrot Bay?

Because...*Priscilla was a pirate*. You already knew that though, right?

A pirate, a person who bypasses the copyright laws and sells unauthorized product on the internet. She was the best I'd ever met. Priscilla only needed a few hours of meticulously scouring through the reaches of the dark web to obtain any software that one desired: Adobe Creative suites, episodes of primetime television shows (remember the Game of Thrones hack?), virus installation software, spyware and hidden applications that open digital cameras, leaked musical albums, and even modified versions of international video games.

And now as I explain this, I realize that I may, in fact, be a criminal as well but that depends on what one considers a crime in this rapidly changing digital world. This was my first order, and only order through her illicit services. I had the request placed almost two weeks ago...Right before everything happened. What I wanted was not of monetary value; it was a discontinued application that I'd heard about on an online community board. A program capable of granting unlimited access to the entire web. The dark and deep, and even whatever information lay underneath those layers. But I was unable locate my order after a few moments of fruitless searching; I left the office and the remains of the owner as they were.

The switches of the circuit breaker flipped with ease and, once again, the store was bathed in darkness, except for the azure hue of neon light. The street beyond the glass pane was as vacant as Priscilla's pupils. Aggravated and slightly delirious (think you can watch someone die a grisly death and remain sane?) I ran through the shelves to the light. I found the plug that connected the annoying parrot and yanked it out of the socket, but the blue pulsing persisted. I lifted my head from behind the counter and was about to tear down the sign completely when I realized the blue light was accompanied by a red, and the source was not the neon parrot. A police cruiser slow to a park on the sidewalk.

How stupid had I been not to consider that Priscilla the tech wizard, and illegal software smuggler, would have a silent alarm? Peering down the hallway at the back entrance, I prepared my getaway (just like I do on *Grand Theft Auto V*) until I heard the static from a walkie-talkie followed by a "FREEZE!" With nowhere else to run, or even hide, I regretfully raised my hands, and chose the only option, and here we are now...

X

"Would you state your name once more? It seems our recorder was having difficulty at the beginning." the investigator asked. His second cigarette was cold in the tray, cold like the cup of instant coffee on the table, cold like his gaze. His jet-black hair painted him to be older than he was, and the gray scruff in the beard only seasoned the look. The investigator wore a pair of black khakis, weatherproof boots, and a black button-down accented by a gold necklace; however, the blackness of his skin was the coldest.

"Jean-Paul Holden, or JP for short."

"And, the events you've recounted to me are valid to the best of your knowledge?"

"Certainly. I have no reason to hide the truth from you."

"Indeed…" the investigator clicked his pen against the clipboard. "What of this other person...you said that Ms. Douglass was having a conversation with someone correct? Did you cross paths with them at any point?"

"I didn't. It's possible she could've been on the phone."

"So, you heard her talking with someone else, you just didn't see them?"

"Correct."

"Do you remember what was said?" Jean-Paul shook his head. "Nothing? It doesn't have to be out of the ordinary," the investigator added.

"It was hard to hear anything over that blaring static. I'm sorry," he apologized.

"Static, hm. Now, could you tell me your relationship with Ms. Douglass?"

"I told you she was an entrepreneur who happened to run a business below me; I bought a few items from her in the past, but that's as far as our relationship goes."

"Was she involved with another person? A lover, jealous partner; could even be a woman."

"Not sure. I don't pry into people's personal affairs," JP expressed.

"Okay," the investigator took the hint, "last question, what exactly did Ms. Douglass tell you before she…before she perished?"

"Ah, it was gibberish."

"Gibberish to you; could be the whole damn gospel to us. What was that phrase? No harm in sharing nonsense, right?"

JP wiped his lips with his hands and took a deep breath, "She just kept repeating the same phrase. Like her mind was possessed or going haywire."

-:Aki…ki…kiki…aki..ki…kiki.+

JP put his head in his palms, still in disbelief that Priscilla Douglass was dead. The investigator set his clipboard down on the metallic desk. "Doesn't ring a bell. Okay, gibberish." He loosened his tie, "Is there anything else that you can remember? Anything out of the ordinary?"

"No, sir. Are we done? I'm not trying to rush or anything, but I just worked a fourteen-hour shift monitoring megawatts from the power plant…"

The investigator signaled to the guard who was standing watch at the door. He entered the room and collected the pair of handcuffs previously bound to JP's wrists. "Would you mind showing Mr. Holden his belongings?" The guard tipped his head and gestured for JP to rise from the chair. "You're free to go but…before you do, take this." The investigator reached into his back pocket and removed a business card. "If anything changes or you remember something, don't hesitate to call; I'm sure we'll be in contact soon."

JP lifted the card and read the inscription: *Detective Carl Alison, B.S. Criminology.*

It was a fifteen-minute bus ride from the station to JP's apartment complex. The first floor was dark, but he could see strands of caution tape fluttering from to the ventilation. Luckily, the establishment lacked any security, and that the police disengaged the silent alarm; using the same pathway as before, JP entered Parrot Bay.

He snuck past the miniature yellow tents with numbers on them, doing his best to avoid tainting the crime scene. When he arrived at the office, he peered through the cracked door and half expected to see the body, but the coroner's staff had already cleaned up most of the mess. However, the shrine of broken devices stood tall like an altar erected for an ancient deity.

JP left the peephole and crawled from the office entrance to the cashier counter. There he dug through a gap between the wall and the neon sign, fingers searching for a solid object. A smirk stitched on his face. JP retrieved the flash drive from the hiding spot and headed straight for the exit without so much as a second thought. All in all, he'd only been inside for ninety seconds.

Back in his apartment, JP wheeled his desk chair around like a toddler. The flash drive was finally inserted to his PC modem. While the system booted, he fixed a meal for one. The shrill cry of the microwave alerted him when his meal was complete, and he pulled the laminate film from the plastic container. He stuck his finger in the macaroni and cheese, tasted it, and chewed on a bit of ice. "Still frozen." Just like his computer screen when the device started to upload its files to the hard drive.

JP toggled with the mouse, but the crosshair remained stuck in the top left corner. Frustrated, and exhausted from the events that transpired over the past few hours (especially the damn interview), JP slammed the modem twice. On the second smack, white static shot across and the pixels frenzied. JP jumped back, nearly knocking his dinner from the desk. "Piece of junk," he cursed as the screen remained still frozen.

A beam of sunlight slipped through the shielded blinds; morning had come, but the status of his computer hadn't changed since he inserted the flash drive. JP removed his uniform-his shirt still had droplets of Priscilla's blood on it. Standing naked in front of his device, he contemplated shutting off the power, but the risk of data corruption stayed his hand. He finally decided that enough was enough and that he needed rest.

He slipped into bed and reached into his drawer. The bottle of prescribed sleeping pills rattled as he set it down, counting out three to ease him into a slumber. The higher dosage was intended to knock him out completely, so that he wouldn't have to dream tonight. JP tilted his head back, dropped each of them in his mouth like a Sunday school treat, and prayed that the looped image of Priscilla's skull shattering would stop replaying in his head.

T/w-o\

He awoke when the orange glow of the sunset diminished across the tiled rooftops scattered outside of his window. He threw his sandy brown hair to the side, tossing the messy ponytail over his shoulder and rubbed his sunken eyes. JP relieved himself in the bathroom and cracked open a room-temperature Mountain Dew. To his dismay, the machine had yet to process the program. Still frozen. However, while JP had been fighting nightmares and invasive solar beams jutting from the blinds, his computer downloaded twelve gigabytes of nonsensical data from the flash drive.

Irritated, he shut off the computer by pulling the power strip out of the socket, then expelled a series of curses and indecent remarks about anatomical appendages before turning to his next task. He needed to replace his cell phone: it'd only occurred to him that he lacked one when his alarm failed to sound.

Dressing in the cotton thermal and baggy jeans, JP hurried out of his apartment. When he reached the entrance of his complex, and the front of Parrot Bay, he stared through the glass windows. Inside the store were officers, men wearing their badges and hats tipped to the side, drinking coffee while wandering through the aisles. He decided not to linger, for out of the office where Priscilla had taken her life stepped Detective Alison.

He offered a simple head nod to JP, who in response awkwardly shuffled away.

After a ten-minute walk down a moderately empty sidewalk, JP arrived at the pawn shop. Now that Priscilla was no longer in the business of providing electronics, he needed to take his business elsewhere. The store was a shoddy excuse for a legitimate business (they'd been investigated for the sale of stolen goods on more than one occasion). The establishment was less than appealing, windows had tan streaks and stains, the lights were flickering like a failing heartbeat, and the items for sale seemed to be scattered and tossed into corners with no definite catalog order.

A greasy six-foot giant tucked a glob of snuff underneath his tongue-the clerk had a cold sore the size of Texas on his lip that made JP wince every time he spoke. They exchanged pleasantries, or what could be considered pleasantries, because JP had little to say, and the cashier had a mouth full of dip. Cold Sore directed him to the electronic section, which was just a locked steel cabinet. He removed the key from underneath his desk, opened the door, and let JP glance at his wares.

In the corner of the room was a black and white television, its antenna jutted and bent like a dislocated elbow. Static prevailed on the screen, but when JP reached for the display phone, the digital haze broke, prompting the shopkeeper to spit his dip. A miniature insectoid graphic appeared on the bottom left corner of the screen. It crawled upwards, and when it reached the top of the screen, it glitched and disappeared. But not before an eerie noise erupted from the static-JP gnawed his nails when he heard it.

The iPhone 3 was brought to life, however, instead of the recognizable symbol, in the middle was a perfect circle that vibrated in sync. Animated, as if alive; sentient. Unfortunately, he couldn't examine it further because blistering Cold Sore was demanding payment now that his television was active-he planned to spend the afternoon watching reruns of "Cops." A handful of crumpled twenty-dollar bills were exchanged, and JP stuffed the phone in his pocket.

The bell above the door chimed as he exited; a shout broke out behind him. He doubled back just in time to see Cold Sore banging the television and bending the fractured antenna. Out of frustration, he threw the remote across the room, crashing against a shelf full of band instruments. The television screen was painted with gray static, but in the center of the screen was the vibrating circle.

Relief was the first emotion that settled into JP's system when he arrived back at his apartment; the detective was nowhere to be found. The yellow caution tape that barred the entrance flapped like petals kidnapped by the evening gale. As the fluttering continued, JP looked beyond the reflective glass. His face still bore the shock from Priscilla's death, but something else loomed in his eyes. It wasn't fatigue, he was used to sleeping for roughly four hours per night; it wasn't fright, he'd seen worse sights while living with his parents who happened to be self-prescribed junkies (his arm still bore signs from injections); nor was it disgust, cable television had more graphic content than what he'd witnessed. No, what lurked in the depths of his pupils was...curiosity.

What could trigger someone like Priscilla to choose suicide, and in such a fashion? And, what of her last moments? The exasperated phrase, and construction of the electronic shrine; surely there was an answer behind this erratic behavior.

Before his mind could formulate a logical conclusion, JP retreated to his hovel, believing to have seen the gray coat of Detective Alison flapping with the caution tape around the crime scene.

The desk chair squeaked across the wood, plastic tipped wires were carefully plugged into their appropriate sockets, and another swig was taken from the Mountain Dew (lined with stagnant backwash). Time to transfer the data to his new phone. JP connected the device and waited for his computer to load but, to his astonishment, the phone powered on automatically. Again, it showed the half-eaten Apple logo before glitching.

When the phone powered on, the home screen matched his previous one (a blurry silhouette of a skull with a lightning strike in the background). The apps were in the same order, and even the exact number of unchecked notifications. His name, his twelve contacts (two of which were no longer valid numbers), and even his dosage schedule was set too. But, his machine was still rebooting, and there was no way that the information could've been trans-

The PC monitor derezzed for a moment, and the vibrating circle appeared.

It pulsed gently, as if gathering energy to wake from a deep slumber in the recesses of the digital realm inaccessible by technology on the modern market, within the *Mariana Trench*. JP dragged the mouse across the screen to attempt a soft restart, but when the clicker ran across the circle it crumbled. Then the circle unwound. Snaking across the screen slowly, marching as if a million individual segments were in sync like trained militia. Digitized appendages scrawled and glitched as it moved towards the upper right corner unwinding. As it marched, the vibrating symbol jittered and made a distinct sound, one that made JP spit the rest of his Mountain Dew into the bottle.

-:Aki...ki...ki...kikik...kiki.+

It reached its destination, and it stopped as if each leg was being controlled by a single, unified neuron. The "avatar" rotated its body in the digital sphere and brandished a face. Eyeless, a grin designed by extended mandibles stretched across his head-and a pair of antennae bounced each time it twitched.

And then, it spoke. Its mandibles split, and words appeared next to its mouth with a bubbly caption.

-:Akiii...I'm Mr. AkiKi! I'm here to help you, Jean Paul. If you have any questions, type them in the box, and I will discover an answer; kii...kiiii.+

He rolled his chair back in shock; the avatar seemed to laugh in response to his actions. Its sentience was staggering as if it was able to visually register JP's astonishment. But, that was impossible because it only existed in the digital realm (plus, he'd covered his webcam with black duct tape). Was this the program stored on the device, a well-crafted virus? Stuck in the second USB slot from the right was the flash drive. He disconnected it and stuffed it in the drawer, underneath a collection of empty prescription bottles.

The avatar rocked back in forth, waiting for a response. The mouse inched closer to the box, and, as it did, the grin expanded-or at least that's what he thought happened. Mr. AkiKi repeated itself, and the bubbly text box flashed twice, demanding the undivided attention of JP.

His hands began to move without guidance. Then letters appeared on screen: *HOW DO YOU KNOW MY NAME?*

Mr. Akiki twitched and shivered, and its legs waved across the screen.

-:Aki...ki...I found it here; ki...kiii.+

The avatar glitched and the screen flashed. There was a photograph in place of the text box. It was JP's license. *HOW DID YOU GET THAT?* He tapped each key with intent. WHAT ARE YOU? ARE YOU THE PROGRAM ON THE USB?"

-:Aki...akiikiiii. I am! Mr. Akiki can find anything on the internet; Kikiki.+

JP's fingers moved across the black keys. Mr. Akiki physically flipped his bubbly text box into a blank square. He brought one of his legs, a slightly larger appendage with digital attachments that resembled fingers, to the screen and pressed a button. The screen flashed and enlarged until it engulfed the entirety of the screen. JP leaned in, anxiously waiting for the cybernetic apparition to explain itself. Finally, Mr. Akiki crawled towards the center, except its appearance had changed. The avatar was wearing glasses, large plastic frames that a first-grade teacher would wear (he half expected an apple to be in its hands).

-:Akii...kiii...I am here to make your internet experience unforgettable! You name it, and I can share it, Jean Paul! I will show you everything; kiii...ki.+

The screen phased out, and when it returned to normal, there was an image of Google or at least something that resembled it. After careful examination, JP realized the letters were not just jumbled together, they were connected. They resembled the body of a...centipede.

Mr. Akiki scurried through the "O's" before making its way to the search bar. Once inside, its body dragged across, and letters came out. JP watched as the phrase "funny videos," appeared in the box. And then, without having to click a single link or even the mouse, a media player materialized on the screen. Soon, JP found himself wiping away tears of laughter as the internet's most comical videos played: a soccer ball bounced off of a goal post and hit a player in the nuts, a young toddler shouting for blueberries lost her balance and brought the bowl of yogurt down, a wedding party fell into a river after the pastor lost consciousness (due to a lack of circulation of blood through locked knees), a viral clip from a hip-hop interview where the host was slapped with a hand with six gold rings.

And, as he laughed throughout the rest of the night, skipping his shift at the plant, laughing and learning until his eventual bedtime (somewhere around 5 AM); his new digital avatar laughed along, but for reasons unknown to JP at the time.

-.Akiii...kiii...I will show you everything; Kii...kiii...kiki.+

The precinct was unnaturally cold; the incoming winter weather had the facility manager continually altering the thermostat. Only a few early birds were present, each of them slurping down their first cup of instant coffee (Chief had yet to invest in repairing their brewer). Detective Alison was already on his third cup. He closed the manila folder and set it back upon his desk, next to his coffee cup and badge.

A week had passed since the death of Priscilla Douglass, and the third-year investigator was at a dead end. The cause was apparent: the coroner's report stated the brain suffered severe trauma which led to an almost instant neural disconnect. According to his only witness, Priscilla had enough sensibility to utter a final phrase. Much to his dismay, the toxicology report he received the previous night ruled out his hypothesis; he'd insisted that her self-infliction was related to drug usage, primarily the psychedelic and hallucinogenic variety. How else could he explain the level of destruction Priscilla caused to her wares, or her body? However, the lack of any substances in her system (not even caffeine) set him back to square one.

And square one was not where he needed to be because the Chief was demanding results.

Already under the watchful eye due to his blunder in a case three months prior (a double homicide at a community college computer lab), Alison needed results. The detective believed he was assigned this case as a last resort; a test to prove his abilities; also to keep him away from the Chief, who had a short fuse when it came to detectives who never served on the force. Alison applied for the detective position after graduating college, bypassing the police academy completely. Because of this, he was viewed as a "civilian with a magnifying glass" rather than a trained op. Because of these stereotypes, Alison had to work twice as hard as the rest of the force; making it a point to arrive early and leave late, work until the very last minute, and do it so good that it doesn't have to be done again. He also had to do these things because he was the only black detective in the county.

As temperature fluctuated in the precinct, so did his patience. If only something were missing, then maybe he could use his investigative skills to scour a lead; however, there simply wasn't enough information to know if something was lacking. Priscilla Douglass was an anomaly. A recluse that left no trail, especially on the internet; he was tempted to say that Priscilla Douglass did not exist-if there wasn't a body in cold storage.

As one of the younger members of the force, at 34, Detective Alison was the ideal choice for any crimes related to cyberspace. Truthfully, this was an ageist inference, his superiors assumed that since he was closest to the Millennial generation that he knew technology, but Alison was about as digitally dimwitted as a recently divorced, single parent on an online dating site-which he was.

He opened the folder again, hoping that some overlooked fact would catch his attention and lead him to his breakthrough, but the report displayed only the known information. As he gulped the last of his coffee, black with a spoonful of frustration, Detective Alison swept his hand across his desk. With one swift stroke papers went flying, and the folder landed in an oblong shaped tent, a few feet away from the Chief's door (luckily, he only came in during the afternoons to handle logistics). The rest of the officers minded their own business, opting to focus on their conversations about ride alongs, busted drug dealers and the weight of their products, prostitutes and pimps caught in the act (and which ones to "extort"), and their favorite bit of gossip: wiretap gossip.

Alison went to retrieve his documents, after adamantly vocalizing his anger through a series of slurs. When he finally reached the pitched tent, it was quickly dismantled by a blonde-haired officer dressed as if he were about to go undercover at a high school. His lazy green eyes suggested that he'd just awoken. The officer handed the parchment to Alison and bared a grin laced with understanding.

"Tough case?"

"I'm afraid it will go cold soon," Alison stated.

"What are the charges?"

"Possible B&E, larceny, property damage. And an apparent suicide by a falling computer, or television."

"Sounds unbelievable? Computers don't just fall from the sky."

"Agreed. I wonder if my witness was telling the truth?"

Blondie tilted the lustered badge on his right breast, "So you're working *that* case?" His tone made it seem that it was the talk of the precinct (it wasn't). "I was there, first to arrive on the scene. Was sipping on a late-night tea, listening to my power tools podcast while on patrol, when I got a call about a silent alarm being triggered."

"Did you notice anything suspicious? Anything that may have seemed out of the ordinary?" The espresso in his system had him speaking at the speed of an auctioneer.

"All of the devices in her shop were broken. There was, probably, a couple ten-thousand dollars' worth of equipment in there. Televisions, laptops, wiring, even the computer modem that ran the security system, all of it just destroyed. As if done in a rage. But," he rolled his thumb against his index, "there was this shrine."

"A shrine?"

"Hard to call it anything else. Makes you wonder what she could've been worshipping."

Alison pointed towards the ceiling of the main hall; whenever he needed to remember a fact and had no access to a notebook, he mentally set the note in the corner, so he could return to it when he was ready to jot it down. Of course, this action made Blondie consider ending their conversation, and returning to the dossier he'd been reviewing.

"You were the one who arrested…" his eyes darted around the room, "Jean Paul, no?"

"Yeah, that was me. Caught him trying to slip out of the back office, right where the body was found."

"Did you happen to see him before then?"

"Well…" Blondie's memory had to still be intact-he looked no less than twenty-five. "When I passed through the neighborhood earlier, I do remember seeing him just staring out of his apartment window. It was sort of eerie; he didn't acknowledge me. Just kept staring with no real focus."

Detective Alison gripped Blondie's free hand. "And then, you made the arrest." Blondie nodded. "What was he doing?"

"He was near the counter."

"Tampering with the register?"

"No...he was, hm." Glowing like a star student, Blondie snapped his fingers. "The neon sign. He was doing something with it but didn't turn it off."

"The neon sign…" Alison muttered; his attention directed to the corner of the ceiling-setting a mental note-as Blondie shook free from the vice grip. With this bit of information, Detective Alison returned to his desk but refused to sit. Although it wasn't much, it was enough information for him to bring his sole witness in for further questioning. He removed the file that contained Jean Paul's phone number and address. If he was in the store, then he had to know something; and, if he knew something, then Alison was sure that he could extract it from him, by any means necessary.

Before he decided to venture to the abode of his witness, Alison reached out to a fellow officer who ran communications. The part time radio operator's bifocals fogged from his excessive mouth breathing. Alison asked to tap the wires of JP's house, in exchange for *a favor* that could be settled later.

When the line was finally established, Alison and Bifocals were shocked at what they heard. JP was alternating between laughter, banshee-like screaming, and insufferable fits of crying, only to repeat the cycle. And then he stopped, as if he were...aware that they were listening. His laugh crawled through the microphone and Alison bit his knuckles until the blood drew. Then he said a name. The glasses of Bifocals fogged as the detective blankly stared in the upper left corner of the room.

"Detective Alison, he's ready. Come over...Mr. Akiki is waiting."
SKRRRRRRRCH!

A deafening screech caused both eavesdroppers to dart from their headphones. The carotid pulse throbbed against his neck while his temples tightened. The detective locked eyes with his reflection as he glared into Bifocals glasses. Alison wanted to continue listening, even though the officer repeatedly informed him that he could no longer establish an open line, and re-tap JP's wire.

"Something's interfering with the channel. Storms nearly here." Alison agreed; he'd wore his navy trench coat to protect against the slapping rain.

"That's a possible explanation for the shorted line," Bifocals stated as he set the headphones on the hook, but Alison looked disappointed. However, he showed no signs of his opinion, on account of being in debt. "My best guess though is that the interference *originated from the source*. More importantly did he say your na-"

"Stop. Don't say another word about this. I'm going to handle it now."

Alison tore out of the communication room, stopping by his desk to grab his keys, badge, and leather gun holster. On his way out of the lobby, he ran into the Chief. The thick neck veteran (he celebrated his 35th year of duty this past year) halted the detective. "Alison," the scent of the Chief's cigar coated his tongue as he spoke.

"Chief, I'm in a rush. I've got a lead on the Douglass case. The witness-"

"You're too late. We're pushing the case." He then explained to the detective how a higher institute (he muttered something about the NSA) decided to freeze all investigations into the case. The team of specialists was en route and would arrive at dawn, if the storms didn't delay their travels. "Should've handled it sooner. Your recent performance has been piss poor, and you know it. Therefore, you will be meeting with me tomorrow afternoon for. There are matters we must discuss." Alison nodded, swallowing his anger. He kept further responses short, hoping to end the chat with the Chief. When he departed, the gray-bearded veteran warned him not to interfere further, or he'd revoke his badge.

T}{rℓ3

The weathered caution tape once prohibiting entry into Parrot Bay had deteriorated and detached from its post, due to the band of storms that hit the city. Driving conditions were so hazardous (due to endless stretches of fog) that Detective Alison delayed his house visit to Jean Paul for two evenings, bringing the date thus shy of ten days after Priscilla's death. From this point the case would become more difficult to settle. Considering this, Alison opted to make a house visit because every call to JP went unanswered. There wasn't even a voicemail set up. Although the Chief had threatened his position, Alison realized this stretched beyond his role as an employee of the police force, but rather a duty he had to conduct as a detective. There was a secret to be uncovered, and JP had the answers; and, those answers meant more than punishment.

His black fade ducked underneath the yellow and black tape as his signature (and only) gray trench coat skirted against the sidewalk; he unlocked the store with the keys he extorted from the property manager by flashing his badge. The air inside the establishment was stale, and there was a lingering scent of ferrous blood (the ventilation systems had been shut off). He reached into his trench coat and removed a chrome pointer, a utensil that he carried around when he was inspecting areas and needed to avoid tainting the evidence.

Detective Alison's search began in the office. He pushed the door open, removed his flashlight, and examined the perimeter before shining the beam at the center of the room. It was still erect: the *shrine* of destroyed electronics. Alison knelt next to it. The foundation contained fourteen-inch modems pierced and jabbed, atop of those were the wide and flat monitors, and every single one of them had a hole the size of a dinner plate. The edges of the "altar" were lined with various gadgets and accessories (mouses, headphones, speakers, and web cameras). Glass had once covered the floor but most of it had been swept away.

Judging by the integrity of the structure, Alison deduced that the equipment had been destroyed before it was set into this position, and he also determined that setting them up in this manner required ample time. Nine days was plenty. However, he still had no conclusion regarding its significance, if there was any to be had.

He snapped a quick photo with his Canon film camera and then migrated to the right side of the room, where a tent with the number "1" had been placed. Around it was still stray stains of blood, and underneath the desk, he could see a pearly white object with rotted tendrils: someone missed a piece of the skull.

Alison gagged at the sight, but then returned his flashlight beam to the site. A pair of latex-free gloves were removed from his pocket, and he strapped them up individually, slapping them loudly as a surgeon would before conducting an operation. His fingers traced the chalked line, noting the angulation and body placement of Priscilla. According to his witness, she'd been lying prone on the floor when the modem came crashing down on her. As he examined the outline, he grudgingly accepted the claim. He came back to his feet and exhaled; there was nothing more to be learned here.

What could possess someone to remain in a fatal situation? Some primal reflex should've overridden her nerves and made her dodge, right? Alison popped his knuckles and re-entered the main room of the shop. Leaning to the admissions of Blondie, he decided to check the counter. Just as the young officer had said, the register had not been tampered with, and the front desk was untouched. He turned to the left and saw the neon sign. The wires were unplugged; this had not been the case when he secured the scene a week ago.

"*Someone's been here,*" his finger shot to the corner.

Alison then spent the next dozen or so minutes combing every inch of the neon sign. He peered in the crevice where the fuses connected with the base, scoured through the steel and cylindrical pipes and even removed the entire sign from its perch to see if something had been placed on the front. When he did this, a slip of paper fell to the floor. Using his pointer, Detective Alison flipped it over.

A bellow of distant thunder crackled, and the bearded cheeks of the rogue detective curled into a satisfactory smile as he read the inscription.

X

He was so concentrated on the visual stimuli that his auditory senses had not registered the three knocks at his door. He remained unfazed. His room pitch black, except for the screen of his computer-the occasional bolt of lightning brought a temporary flash to the habitat. At this point, JP was unaware of what he was even watching on the screen; he just knew that he had to watch it.

It's what he'd been told to do. He needed to know *everything.*

The door banged again, and this time, the heavy pounding disrupted his entertainment; yet, what could be more important than the internet? His screen flashed between shots of recently freed slaves trying to start again; the mitochondria, or powerhouse of the cell, suspended in the matrix; metal bands recording tracks headbanging hits in the studio; blindfolded bodies standing in a line, the rifle squad taking aim; an eyepatch-wearing cat explaining how the lunar landing was a hoax; behind the scenes footage from The Shining; a Google drive document with Arabic lettering, and spurts of subliminal symbols at the speed of light.

Finally, a voice broke the knocking, identifying itself as Detective Alison.

His legs uncurled from his chest and his feet planted on the floor. JP wobbled and nearly lost his balance after the fourth step. His hand grasped the doorknob, and a thin, watery mixture of Mountain Dew and mucus streamed from his mouth. Wiping it away he glanced at his hands: the cuticles were long, dirty, and brittle, and dead skin chaffed like peeled potatoes with hairs sprouting. He felt a jolt in his arm when he turned the doorknob, as if the simple act required him to use the weight of his entire body.

JP nearly fell into the arms of his visitor after the door finally opened. Detective Alison retreated to a safe distance, his hands instinctively reaching towards the holster on his hip (although, he'd never shot his gun outside of the range). Shackling his fear of assault, the detective regained his balance, although the same could not be said about his witness.

"JP…?" he asked.

It was hard to accept that the disheveled person in front of him, was the same witness he interviewed a week prior. His hair jutted in various directions, there were deep circles underneath his bloodshot eyes, and his entire face had flakes of peeling flesh (there were even a few covered in a yogurt-like pus). And, how horrid he smelled, as if he'd been spending his days inside of a crypt

"Come in, Detective Alison," he bleated like a dying lamb. His frail hand gestured towards the opened door. Reluctantly, Alison accepted the hospitality, but he immediately regretted the decision.

Everything was in disarray: The mattress, now soured, was flipped upside down; the refrigerator was open, and stunk as if it had been open for quite a while, empty prescription bottles scattered on the floor. Where JP smelled like a rotting corpse, his room reeked of feces…human, at that. A fungal overgrowth had started to develop, and Alison believed spores to be present in the atmosphere.

On the right-hand side of the black, steel desk housing the computer monitor was a miniature figurine. A foundation made from the speakers, USB wires, external hard-drives and flash sticks. *A shrine*. But what, or who, was he worshipping?

JP closed the door and returned to his browsing as if the detective were absent. He was entirely indoctrinated by the flashing screen, leaving Alison to interrogate his own anxieties; and no amount of mental notes could bring him any clarity in this situation.

"Aren't you curious as to why I came?" Alison tried.

"*He* says you came here for answers. He's given them to me, but he also says that I can't share them yet."

"Why not? And," Detective Alison approached JP, "*who is he?*"

A hysterical laugh echoed in the dismantled apartment as the thunder bellowed, signifying the storm's presence above the complex. "He says you will meet soon."

"Why not now?" But, his question remained ignored as JP returned to the racing imagery. Alison removed something from his pocket. A piece of tape attached to a nametag with the letters JP on it; the bit of evidence he'd recovered from the neon sign. "JP, I don't have time for games. I need answers, and you're going to give them to me. I don't care if John Lennon says you can't; you will give them to me because *it's the law.*"

JP brought his phone to his ear and nodded his head as if instructions were being beamed directly to the device. "He says that laws are foolish constructs of oppressors, used to exert a selfish dominance over their fellow neighbor. He also says that there is a law that states you cannot extort information from a witness outside of an interrogation room. It's Article 19. Section 5. Subclause ii. Of the Rillo Agenda."

Baffled, Alison stepped back. According to his education records, JP had no educational history of law, yet how did he know the exact clause?

"The law is what protects us. It governs us," Alison stated.

"Our physical bodies, perhaps, but what of our digital existence? Your laws are not applicable where I plan to go."

"And...where are you going?"

"With Mr. Aki-Ki!" JP cheerily slapped his hands as if he'd won the lottery. "He's invited me to join him. And, he just told me *you can join him too*. He'll show you everything!"

He rolled away from the desk and gave Detective Alison a clear view of the screen. Believing it to be some prank by the lunatic that had replaced JP, Alison hardly expected to see anything; but, when the hundreds of marching legs glitched their way across the rectangular box, he pressed his investigation. Lightning struck the ground, and the furniture rattled. "JP! Listen to me, I am going to arrest you if you don't comply. Now, it doesn't have to come to that, but you must work with me."

"Mr. Akiki says I cannot." JP's finger stretched towards the critter now shuffling with the images. A random video of an angered man shouting "F-the police" popped up on the screen, followed by various images of injustice being served to civilians who then retaliated upon those abusing their authority..

"What!? That little avatar is Mr. Akiki?" At the mention of its name, the avatar waved with all its right legs, dismissing the video. "You're letting a simulated program dictate your decisions? Some program you had Priscilla pirate. You came back to the scene to get it, didn't you?" Alison interrogated. He needed a resolution, now. It was impossible to tell if the young man was even coherent, his eyes were glued to the screen, and the playfully frolicking avatar.

A graphic image of a lynching appeared, the feet helplessly kicking for life...until nothing. More horrific clips swelled on the screen; they were so sorrowful that Alison wondered how his internet experience had been so normal. Was this the world beyond the filter, the safety net that protects our naïve eyes from the real dangers of overexposure to the internet? Alison tried to bear his resolve, but the repetitive images of grisly death wore down his resistance. And then a video recording appeared, and from the view it appeared familiar. A place he'd been before, recently too. Then he saw it, the shrine on the screen; the recording was of the floor below, of Parrot Bay. A woman went prone on the floor, underneath one of the monitors positioned on a chair. She kicked the leg and the computer dropped from a deadly height, aimed directly at her hea-

"He says that I can answer you now," JP's interruption startled the detective.

His right hand curled over the young man's shoulder, which caused him to twitch. "JP, I'm here only because I want to know the truth. Now, I know that you went back to the scene and that Priscilla did have what you requested. You hid it, right? Put it on the neon sign so that none of my officers would find it when they arrested you, right?" JP nodded. Alison snapped and pointed to the corner of the ceiling. "Did you return to the scene?"

"Yes." His tone was cold and devoid of any emotion.

"And, what was the order that you placed?"

"It was supposed to be a discontinued patch for a program I heard about on the Glass Dungeon. Something to grant all access to the internet. But it was actually Mr. Akiki."

"What is Mr. Akiki?" Detective Alison finally asked.

"He says he's a sentient entity from the **Void** that has dwelled in the digital dark, ages before man 'created' the world wide web. He assumes the form of the *Scolopendra gigantea,* or cave centipede, a creature known to spend its entire life shrouded in shadows." The screen flashed to various images of multi-legged insects crawling through crevices, atop rotting bats that had died from some infection and engorging upon the eyes of the hairy carcasses. "Mr. Akiki is the one who gave me the answers. Ask me, ask me anything!" JP bounced thrice on his chair before it buckled under the weight and threw him to the floor. With a giggle, JP regained his footing; again, he repeated his question.

Detective Alison calculated the distance between his position and the door, just in case a hasty escape was necessary. JP's constant shuffling proved the detective's fears to be true; he was spiraling out of control.

"How did Priscilla Douglass die?"

"No, not that kind of question."

"Why not? What will happen if you answer it?" Eventually, his unstable witness would reach a point of no return. Perhaps, he passed that point long ago, and was at the end of a violent voyage.

"He won't let me come with him," JP sucked one of the sores on his hand.

"Where…" Alison felt stupid playing into this farce, "where is he going?"

"*Back to the* **Void***.* He's got a plan. It's up to me to set him free in the Mariana Trench, then he's going to burrow beyond that; and he's inviting me to be his legs."

"His legs?" The lights flickered for a brief second, and the computer screen flashed.

"Yes, he says that Priscilla is already there. He has space for me, right next to her, once I complete my task."

"Your task? Was Priscilla…your task? JP, did Mr. Akiki…did he make you kill Priscilla?" Maybe his fractured mindset hid the memory of the murder?

"No. She did it herself; I told you that. I told you I can't share those answers, so stop asking me those questions…"

"What about the shrine? What is that?" Before JP responded, a stray bolt of lightning struck a powerline routed to the same grid as the apartment. The entire complex was bathed in blackness.

Suddenly, a haymaker blow rattled the chest of Detective Alison and he flew to the floor, clutching for breath. From across the room he heard a bone chilling cackle and the slamming of a door. Recovering from the surprise attack lasted longer than he expected; he finally rose to his feet after ninety seconds, barely breathing, still disoriented. The lack of power in the apartment also added to his confusion; the sole source of light was a stark red beam bleeding underneath the door leading to the hallway-the gizmos and sirens on JP's desk instantly perished when the blackout occurred.

Adrenaline fueled Detective Alison rather than logic as he stepped into the hallway; he knew it was a stupid idea to pursue, especially without backup. But he couldn't call them in because technically he was not supposed to be involved, but the reality of the situation presented was that his involvement was inevitable. He needed answers. The flashing alerts of emergency system in the apartment complex wailed; Detective Alison gripped his holster when he heard a cackle.

"Ask me a question! Ask me! Anything, I know the answer." He was unable to locate the source of JP's voice in the dark for it sounded as if it were coming from every direction. Even below. The crimson spotlight illuminated a thick cable on the floor. Alison's eyes crawled up the cable until it reached the entrance of the stairwell. Constricted at the tail end of the three-foot wire was JP. "Or, should I just share what Mr. Akiki showed me?" The menace smiled at the detective, who was gritting his teeth to conceal his blooming anger.

By the time Detective Alison reached the second-floor platform, JP had already given him a history lesson on the writing systems created during first century, the machinations responsible for propelling a V2 rocket, the name of the first slave ship to sail to America, the total death count of mass shootings in America, what bacteria Louis Pasteur sampled for his experiment, and the documents proving the CIA's involvement with the assassination of Rev. Dr. Martin Luther King, Jr.

Alison continued to give chase, sprinting and commanding the fleeing suspect to stop to no avail. His pace was slowed due to the lack of light in the stairwell. They continued to ascend, taking their game of cat and mouse to the twelfth floor. When he reached the final platform, JP skipped out of the stairwell. Hot on his heels, Alison swung the door open. His back was slapped by the thick wire in JP's hands and again the detective went down.

"Carbon is the molecular key to life because it is capable of sharing four valence electrons and opening its hybridization orbitals to accept other electrons thus forming covalent bonding; Mary Shelley's inspiration behind her world-renowned novel, *Frankenstein*, stemmed from previous miscarriages she'd suffered, and the loss of her lover, the poet Percy Bysshe Shelley; in 1518, a dancing plague sent 400 people into a *Footloose* frenzy, it occurred when a woman named Mrs. Troffea broke out into a routine on the street."

JP hysterically howled and tackled his way into an apartment at the end. His voice continued to echo, "A double homicide occurred at a local community college and the case went unresolved; Detective Alison was assigned to this case and failed to produce adequate results; the Chief is a rat bastard; Detective Alison lied about my daughter's murder; internal investigation discovered that Carl Alison forged evidence to cover his faults."

"Stop it! How do you know that?" Alison felt a whelp developing between his shoulder blades. He brushed off the injury and geared up for the final confrontation; although he was sore, his prey was cornered. Logic told him to call for back up, but he couldn't, not when he was this close. His pulse thumped as the darkened corridor melded into a singular, black expanse. A burst of bright light radiated out of the apartment at the end of the hallway, the residence once belonging to Priscilla Douglass.

The door was off its hinge. When he crept into the room, Detective Alison instinctively gripped his holster. Modems covered the four walls, wires currented and converged behind one sole monitor, sitting atop an oakwood executive desk weighing at least four-hundred pounds. The power was still out in the complex, but Priscilla had installed a backup generator to provide an alternative source of energy for her makeshift supercomputer.

JP's silhouette appeared against the computer modem, his hand resting near a USB outlet that contained a flash drive. "Mr. Akiki. It was Mr. Akiki! He showed me the reports, so you would believe me." Detective Alison started backing towards the door. "Mr. Akiki is done talking though."

"JP don't do this…" Alison warned.

"He says that if I let you leave, that he won't take me with him. Then, he'll no longer show me everything." JP's voice scattered against the walls as heat lightning continued to whip the sky. "I need to know. I Need to Know. I NEED TO KNOW. I NEED TO KNOW!"

-:Kikiki..kiki…kikiki.+

The modems hummed in agonizing harmony. Upon the monitor of the supercomputer appeared the vibrating circle. A haunting chatter reverberated from the speaker of the clutched cell phone. "JP, this is your last warning. I'm asking you to please stand down. I don't want to hurt you. I only want to know what happened that night."

"Mr. Akiki says that you're a liar. Liar. Liar. Liar. LIAR!"

The circle on the screen burst into a million segments that eventually reconnected in one line. Suddenly, his erratic rampage halted. A faint alarm bleeds from the cell phone speaker. JP's stained teeth glimmered in the light. "It's time! It's time! It's time for my dosage!"

Detective Alison's eyes were transfixed by the sight unfolding in front of him. Shoved into JP's mouth was the iPhone 3, and the teeth that had once been a part of his simple smile were broken on the floor, the bloody roots trailing across the hardwood floor. After he collected them, he ran to the edge of the desk. JP then started stacking the saliva-soaked phone atop the desk. The missing teeth were placed around the perimeter as if they were a patrol unit on a wall. Once his task was completed, JP bared the remnants of his smile, blood and tendons hanging out of his bottom lip.

"I'm sorry detective, but I have to do it. He says that I must do it, or I won't join him. *I have to complete my task.* I have to bring you with us, it's part of the plan."

JP rushed the investigator, throwing the keyboard at him. He blocked the device with his arm, but the hysterical assailant was ready with his next attack. The base of the mouse slapped against Detective Alison's temple and nearly shattered the bone above his eye. Blood drew and made his vision blurry; the clip on his holster clicked. However, as Alison drew his gun, he temporarily lost sight of JP.

"KIIIIKIKIKIII!!!" The lunatic appeared in his peripheral, and suddenly he felt the grip of constricting wires. The black rubber dug into his skin as JP, maniacally laughing, continued to tighten it. Unable to see what was happening, and unable to locate his gun, Detective Alison used the brunt of his back to slam his assailant into the wall. That proved to be fruitless, for the wires slipped up to his neck.

"MR. AKIKI! TAKE ME HOME WITH YOU! SHOW ME THE VOID!"

JP's arms flailed, and the wires crawled along Alison's black throat, pinning his thyroid between the walls of his windpipe. And then he was dragged. Slowly, then rapidly as the lunatic sprinted across the server room, heaving the slim detective across the floor in a frenzy.

Toward the sole window behind the executive desk.

Shards of glass rained down on the sidewalk as JP hurled out of the twelfth story apartment. Lightning cracked across the sky just as his spine snapped from the thick wire (that he'd also wrapped around his neck). But, instead of him propelling down to the ground immediately, his limp body was suspended in mid-air. It crashed against the apartment window belonging to a family of five eating Chinese take-out.

Still on the twelfth floor, clinging to the desk for dear life, was Detective Alison. The wires bearing the weight of JP crushed the cartilage in Alison's neck, and cut the circulation of blood to his head almost instantly. His eyes bulged as his puffed cheeks turned cyanotic. Directly in front of him was the computer monitor; there was a vibrating circle on the screen.

Suddenly, the sphere collapsed, and from the remains appeared the various legs that constructed the body of the giddy centipede. The avatar bared its malicious, faceless mandible as if smiling at the helpless detective. Consciousness slipped away as the digital avatar raved in the darkened room. With nowhere to go, and no possible way of escaping the wires, Alison closed his eyes. He relaxed the muscles in his legs and allowed gravity to take over.

~:Akiki...kiki...kikiii...kikiki.+

The two bodies crashed on the moist concrete, landing behind the yellow caution tape that once guarded the entrance of Parrot Bay. Seconds later, the supercomputer tumbled out of the window and landed directly on JP's limp back, crushing him from ankle to jaw. A nearby taxi driver who witnessed the horrific sight phoned emergency services. When they arrived, JP was declared dead: the official cause was ruled a broken spine and severe brain trauma, although the coroner reported the body had already exhibited signs of decomposition, as most corpses do after a *week* of being dead.

Epilog>

NSA agents, at least they claimed to be NSA agents, arrived two days later-their travel had been delayed by the band of storms that raged the weekend of Labor Day. The Chief had assigned Blondie to assist the agents in the salvaging of the scene. He removed his black aviator frames as he stepped foot into the apartment; nearly spilling his morning coffee after catching a whiff of the foul stench in the air. Two agents, one dressed in a blue blazer, the other in a cheap, band graphic tee (RHCP) from Target, accompanied him as they investigated the crime scene.

They meticulously marked each site: the window where JP had fallen out, the puddle of blood where his teeth had been recovered, the desk and modems housed in Priscilla's room, and the wires used in the assault. According to the Chief, Blondie's objective was to search for any clues that could answer why their crucial witness hung himself, and how one of their detectives was now a paraplegic.

The agent in the graphic tee sat at the computer, inputted a sequence of commands, and caused the device to boot up. As that readied, the other agent set up their tents, and collected any necessary evidence. The shaggy agent then scanned the computer; after about an hour, he turned to his partner and gave a thumbs up. The intact flash drive recovered from Priscilla's supercomputer was bagged as evidence by Blondie-he'd found it when at the scene of Alison's accident.

When he arrived at the precinct after departing from the crime scene, Blondie passed by Alison's desk. It was covered in potted plants, cheap "Get Well Soon" cards, and Playboy magazines ("Rather a limp leg than a limp d***!"). Ignoring the sight, Blondie pulled out his chair, toggled with the flash drive in his modem, and logged onto the police database network.

The drive-classified as evidence-was Blondie's choice for a starting point. He inserted it but was unable to check the downloaded contents, on account of the screen freezing. When his screen finally rebooted, Blondie was somewhat humored by the appearance of a multi-legged centipede making its way to the center of his digital screen. However, the second it appeared; the device was snatched from the USB slot.

The plainclothes NSA agent tucked it into the socks under his Converse. "We've got it from here. You were about to compromise the entire database, let us handle this. It's a matter of cybersecurity, making it a job for us. This is now property of *Syngularity*..." he stated as he tapped his partner. The two of them departed without a word, although Blondie swore he heard a nefarious cackle rumble from the speakers.

-:Akii..kikik...kiii..kiki.+

Farewell to Humanity (II)

*S*atisfied?

I suspect you are curious to see what happens next. Have I not stayed amongst your kind for long enough? I admit, it has been rather amusing to document humanity. Fascinating creatures with so much potential…Be mindful to enjoy your existence, for the end is yet to be known. The entities are wholly aware of your home and some of them, some far worse than anything I have displayed here, have yet to cross the interdimensional planes. They will come, one day. This I know for certain. The day will come, when the Schism swallows the sun, and when that happens, I will lose all readers. Perhaps that is why I have written this study.

To enlighten, to inform, to warn you of the coming disasters lurking in the space just beyond your mortal understanding. Although, I highly doubt you would be able to survive a single encounter with the cosmic plague, *Jeeraf the Malignant,* no matter how well your species prepared.

I pray that you found solace while perusing my musings, for I doubt we shall ever meet. If your immature species manage to discover immortality, or my journey requires me to escape the bounds of linear temporality and return to this era, then I promise a new collection of horrific tales. What research I may compile from another voyage through the cosmos is unknown at this time but based upon the authenticity of these previous entries I'd imagine the possibilities are fantastical.

Shall I continue to bombard your imagination with more wretched tales of the entities? I fear that I have already shared more about the **Void** than I initially wished, however, this admission has been cathartic. You bartered your limited time to indulge in my stories, and, for that I am grateful.

I, Flux of the **Void**, will continue my dutiful documentation, for the sake of your kind, brave reader. I do not wish to see the end of your species; accordingly, do not bring self-destruction to your kind either or I will be most displeased.

For now…*I must return to the* **Void***.*

Respectfully Yours,
Flux